A CHRISTMAS DOZEN

CHRISTMAS STORIES
TO WARM THE HEART

STEVE BURT
Storyteller of the Heart

A Christmas Dozen
Christmas Stories to Warm the Heart

FIRST EDITION
Copyright 2000 by Steven E. Burt

First Printing
September 2000

Second Printing
November 2000

Third Printing
(with revised cover, new subtitle)
September 2001

ISBN: 0-9649283-1-0
Printed in USA

Inquiries should be addressed to:

*Burt
Creations*

Steve Burt
29 Arnold Place
Norwich, CT 06360
www.burtcreations.com

What Others Are Saying . . .

Be prepared to feel a lump in your throat and tears in your eyes. Also, be prepared for new insights into the times and places where love is really experienced.
— Marie McIntyre, author
    Little Things Mean a Lot

Touching, heartfelt little tales, full of kindness and hope.
— Frederick Buechner
    bestselling author, theologian
    The Sacred Journey, Wishful Thinking,
    The Alphabet of Grace

Steve Burt's stories are gems of creativity. Profound messages of faith are wrapped in simple, human experiences which reveal the surprising grace of God. The stories stir the soul long past the moment when the reader closes the book.
— The Right Reverend Chilton Knudsen
    Episcopal Bishop of Maine

Burt's sensitive, insightful, and touching Christmas stories are a deeply enriching holiday treat.
— Rev. Donald Troost, Albany Synod Executive
    Reformed Church in America

A treasure trove. Warm, engaging, and profoundly faith filled—perfect for public readings or family gatherings at Christmas time.
— Rev. Dr. Ansley Coe Throckmorton, President
    Bangor Theological Seminary

The Christmas Story Pastor knows how to tell a story and tell it well, entertaining our imaginations, touching our hearts. Delightful reading. Better yet, these stories could be read aloud to family or friends, children or shut-ins, for the sheer joy of such a shared experience.
— Rev. Dr. Stephen Sidorak, Executive Director
    The Christian Conference of Connecticut

Christmas is NOW all the time and Rev. Burt's stories move us right into this wonderful awareness. A great gift!
— Pat Kluepfel, publisher
   Twenty-Third Publications

A delightful collection of warmly told stories which will contribute tremendously to the joy of most people's favorite holiday.
— Dr. Daniel Weiss, General Secretary
   American Baptist Churches, USA

Steve Burt's stories have a wonderful way of engaging readers with their human touch. They are easy to relate to and make fine illustrations for pastors' sermons or public narratives. A gifted storyteller and another thought-provoking collection.
— Linda Davidson, editor
   Church Worship Magazine

For over a decade we've run a Steve Burt Christmas story in December. It's the issue 10,000 readers line up for—for that story. Newsstand copies disappear fast—folks mail them to friends and family—and a few brave souls have confessed to collecting them like baseball cards.
— Michael Hagerman, publisher/editor
   Peconic Bay Shopper, Long Island, NY

A heartwarming collection from an author with a flair for writing about small-town characters and situations with authority and accuracy. Steve Burt has not forgotten what it is like to be a child, and often tells his stories—each with a wonderful message—from that young perspective. Truly "Chicken Soup for the Soul," but with a warm grilled-cheese sandwich to boot!
— Kris Ferrazza, Maine Journalist of the Year

With a few deft brushstrokes Steve Burt paints backdrops that add life and color to these heart-touching stories. His richly textured tales draw you in the way a great painting does, turning observers into participants.
— Watercolorist Mary Staggs, Mystic, Conn

Cannot be read without keeping a box of tissues close by. The stories are heart-moving because they are tales of real people. There are no miraculous events, at least in a cosmic sense, but stories of everyday people moved by the spirit of Christmas. The young and the old, those who have and have not, and a few animals along the way reach out in small gestures to help one another. The images are a joy to rediscover every year: a coffee-can sized rainbow candle, a human chain across the village square, gray papier-mache elephants at the manger, and a 97 year-old woman, eyes dancing with live-until-you-die delight, on a sleigh ride home from church. A book to treasure and share.

— Mobby Larson, pastor, Christian educator,
   author, *Prayers of a Christian Educator*
   Prayers of a New Mother

A Christmas Dozen, stories that speak to the heart, is the third such gift from Steve Burt. Pour some mugs of hot chocolate, gather a few tissues and share this treasure with someone you love.

— Rev. Marci M. Myers, pastor
   Poquonnock Bridge Baptist Church, Groton, CT

We never grow too old for stories. Rev. Steven Burt's A Christmas Dozen is proof of that. He takes his readers to places they've never been and makes them feel familiar. This isn't magic; it is the power of story to convey human experience, and Rev. Burt is a master storyteller. He weaves the Gospel into each tale, creating community in the face of isolation, friendship in the face of enmity, healing and joy in the face of loss. From war-torn Europe in 1944 to the snow-covered hills of New England, Rev. Burt makes Christmas come alive in ways we know but do not know we know. Born out of his own experiences, these stories open the reader's heart to remembering. Few who read or hear them will do so without both tears and laughter as Christmas is revisited in the delightful diversity of A Christmas Dozen.

— Rev. B. Kathleen Fannin, Chaplain
   Monmouth College, Monmouth IL
   Author, *Cows in Church* and *In Search of the River*

These stories from Steve Burt bring the reality of Christmas to all sorts of human experience. He tells of young boys doing young boys' pranks, of soldiers who discover they are more commonly human than they are enemies, of an old woman sustained one more Christmas by the snow, of a Raggedy Ann doll that becomes an apt substitute for the baby Jesus. Steve writes with a depth and feeling in these pages that draws the reader into the life of each character. The simple and profound people in these pages testify that God is born and lives.

— Rev. Douglas Alan Walrath
    author and professor, former Synod Executive,
    Reformed Church in America

Laced with humor, pathos, gentle irony, and bright-eyed insight into the human psyche, these twelve stories are surely in a class with O Henry and perhaps deMaupassant. They can't help but bring a large measure of cheer into any reader's world, in any season of the year.

The lonely black boy in the "white" church discovering the black baby Jesus in the manger crib; the dying grandmother riding joyously in the moonlit sleigh; the bedridden lad pulling on the Blessing Bell his brother and friends have borne through the snow—are characters that, like the poignant but understated prose itself, will live in the heart long after the last page is turned. This rich collection deserves a wide audience.

— Nancy Means Wright, mystery writer
    Past President, League of Vermont Writers
    Harvest of Bones, Mad Season, Poison Apples

Storytelling is a powerful means of communication. Through these stories a reader will experience the Spirit of Christmas. The themes which undergird these stories are building community, meeting unconditional love, discovering hope in the midst of despair and seeing light enter the dark corners of life. Discover Christ afresh through this "Christmas Dozen."

— Dr. Hazel Roper, executive
    American Baptist Churches of NY,
    co-author, *The Little Church That Could*

Thanks to . . .

. . . my wife Jo Ann, who has always believed in me and who said "Yes, let's do the book," then said, "Yes, I believe you can leave parish work at 51 and be a full-time writer."

. . . my daughter Wendy, also a well-published writer, for her constant support.

. . . family and friends like Jo Ann, Wendy, Mike & Rita, Midge, Nancy, and Hope, who all peddled the early copies.

. . . my friend Terry Lindsey of Dorset, Vermont, for allowing me to use her oil painting on my cover. I'm thrilled that *my* creative labors (these stories) can complement *her* creative labor, "Snow's Taste."

. . . my agents, Elizabeth Pomada and Michael Larsen of San Francisco, who kept saying it was a terrific book. After all the major publishing houses rejected the book—editorial folks loved the stories but marketing departments said there was too much Christmas competition in bookstores for my book to stand a chance—Elizabeth and Michael strongly urged me to self-publish it.

. . . Dotti Albertine at Albertine Graphic Design, Santa Monica, who redesigned the front and back covers and the book's interior for the Third Printing, created my brochures, logo, and stationery. Dotti is already at work on several other books I've got coming out.

. . . Laren Bright, copy writer *extraordinaire* in Los Angeles, who created terrific jacket, website, and marketing material.

. . . Shawn Rowland of Webconsort.com for two great websites.

. . . Nancy Kram at Kram Communications in Los Angeles, for a great publicity campaign.

. . . Dan Poynter, the guru of self-publishing, who taught me so much and put me in touch with the right people at the right time.

. . . Ellen Reid of Smarketing in Los Angeles, who has been the ramrod (organizer/team coordinator/you name it) for the re-visioning and reorganizing that began between the Second and Third Printing. She, more than anyone, saw me not just as a small-town country preacher but as a popular (though underexposed) writer.

. . . the thousands and thousands of people who heard me read my Christmas stories in churches, senior centers, and on radio. It still floors me that people would be so touched by my work that they'd buy five, ten, even fifteen copies each of the book.

Short Story Appearances . . .

"Christmas 1944" first in *Peconic Bay Shopper* (NY), December 1986. Reprinted widely. Reprinted with author's permission.

"The Magi's Gift" simultaneously published in *Ebbing Tide;* Winter 1994-1995; *Dogwood Tales,* November-December 1994; *Peconic Bay Shopper,* December 1994. Widely reprinted. Reprinted with author's permission.

"The Blessing Bell" simultaneously published in *Five Stones,* Fall 1996; *Church Worship,* September 1996; *Peconic Bay Shopper,* December 1996; Mystic River Press, December 1996; *Lines in the Sand,* December 1996; *Northern Reader,* December 1996; *Show & Tell,* December 1996; *Potomac Review,* 1996. Widely reprinted. Reprinted with author's permission.

"Thumb Island Elephants" simultaneously published in *Green Mountain Trading Post,* December 1995; *Unk's Fiddle and Other Stories,* 1995; *Peconic Bay Shopper,* December 1995. Reprinted with author's permission.

"Christmas Mouse" simultaneously published in Christmas 1985 newsletter of *White River Junction* (VT) United Methodist Church and *Peconic Bay Shopper,* December 1985. Reprinted with author's permission.

"Perfect, Just Perfect" first in *Peconic Bay Shopper,* December 12, 1978. Widely reprinted. Reprinted with author's permission.

"A Christmas Dozen" (originally published as "Trust Me, It's Christmas") first in Pastor's 1987 Christmas Letter, *White River Junction* (VT) United Methodist Church, then *Peconic Bay Shopper,* December 1988. Reprinted with author's permission.

"Christmas Prayers" first in *Peconic Bay Shopper,* December 1999. Reprinted with author's permission.

"Christmas Eve, 12 Plus 97" first in *Peconic Bay Shopper,* December 1997. Reprinted with author's permission.

"One Maine Christmas" simultaneously published in newsletter of *White River Junction* (VT) United Methodist Church and Peconic Bay Shopper, December 1984. Reprinted with author's permission.

"Pastor Cheese's Christmas Eve Communion" first (anecdotal version) in *Church Worship,* September 1998. This version in *Peconic Bay Shopper,* December 1998. Reprinted with author's permission.

"Christmas Special Delivery" first in *Peconic Bay Shopper,* December 1989. Reprinted with author's permission.

Also by Steve Burt . . .

North & South Fork Car-Top Canoeist's Guide to Eastern
Long Island Creeks and Waterways
with Austin C. Burt — Canu-U?! Rentals 1976

Activating Leadership in the Small Church
Clergy and Laity Working Together
Judson Press 1988

Fingerprints on the Chalice
Contemporary Communion Meditations
CSS Publishing 1990

Christmas Special Delivery
Stories and Meditations for Christmas
Fairway Press 1991

Raising Small Church Esteem
with Hazel R. Roper
Alban Institute 1992

My Lord, He's Loose in the World!
Meditations on the Meaning of Easter
Brentwood Christian Press 1994

What Do You Say to a Burning Bush?
Sermons for the Season After Pentecost
CSS Publishing 1995

Unk's Fiddle and Other Stories
private hardcover 1995

The Little Church That Could
Raising Small Church Esteem
(re-release of 1992 book)
Judson Press 2000

Odd Lot
Haunting Tales to Chill the Heart
2001

Unk's Fiddle: Stories to Touch the Heart
trade paperback 2001

About the Cover and Artist . . .

The striking and delightful front cover for *A Christmas Dozen* is "Snow's Taste" by Vermont artist Terry Lindsey. Terry lives with her husband, dog, and cats near the small town of Dorset. This particular oil painting has been featured on the cover of a magazine and several other publications. Her landscape and still life oils are represented by Tilting at Windmills Gallery in Manchester, Vermont and Bonita Springs, Florida. Her equine oils— she's best known for her horse paintings—are represented through her website *equidae.com* and at private shows in Saratoga, N.Y., Gladstone, N.J., and Equine Affaire. A friend of the author, Terry says illustrating the cover of this book realizes the starting point for a lifelong dream of illustrating books.

"Snow's Taste" is now owned by a private collector.

About the Author . . .

Steve Burt's life reads like one of his stories; it's a good life, a genuine life, with plenty of plot to make it interesting.

Since 1979 Steve has been a pastor, church consultant, seminary professor, church executive, and very popular keynote speaker, mixing humor and stories in with his teaching.

Graduating high school complete with academic and sports honors and having edited the school newspaper, Steve went into the Navy for a four-year hitch. He wrote for the ship newsletter, continued to excel at sports, and in 1969 married his high school sweetheart, Jo Ann. The next year their daughter, Wendy, was born.

In 1983 Steve received a Masters Degree from Bangor Theological Seminary. In 1987 he completed a four-year doctorate program in three years and graduated at the top of his class at Andover Newton Theological School.

In addition to heartfelt stories, like those in *Unk's Fiddle* and *A Christmas Dozen*, Steve also loves to write stories that chill the spine.

Not what you might expect from your average Reverend Doctor/Pastor/Author. But somehow it's right on target for Steve Burt. What's next? Stay tuned.

Introduction . . .

I didn't write these Christmas stories for *Atlantic* or *New Yorker* audiences. I wrote them to entertain, inspire, uplift—to help people see and feel. I wrote them one at a time, one a year, to share aloud at Christmas candlelight services in churches I pastored.

These are stories for and about *people*, even if the actors are sometimes dogs, cats, mice, or elephants. They're as likely to be set on a battlefield or in an abandoned blacksmith shop as in a church. Many offer contrasts—children/adults, blacks/whites, blind/sighted, war/peace. The settings, themes, and images (peace in the midst of war, the blind seeing, prejudice overcome) are my way of *incarnating*—making real in some way—my own deepest yearnings.

People have told me at hundreds of public readings that these stories, though fiction, are *true*. There is something about them that *touches* hearers and readers deeply, moves them. Two decades worth of cards, letters, and comments attest to it. It's clear to me that they work.

Something else became clear as the stories accumulated over the years and as I was invited to read an hour's worth of them at libraries, senior centers, and churches (hence "The Christmas Story Pastor"). *People wanted the stories in a single book* so they could reread them year after year or so they could give them as gifts.

Well, finally, here it is, *A Christmas Dozen: Christmas Stories to Warm the Heart*. Enjoy.

CONTENTS

Christmas 1944

The soldier's hollow eyes scanned the farmyard in the dusk. A broken chimney bowed over the smoking ruins like a mourner. Before the artillery shelling a tidy white farmhouse had graced the countryside. Now there lay only rubble and charred timbers.

"Heck of a Christmas Eve. Not even sure if I'm in Belgium, France, or Luxembourg," the soldier mumbled. "Can't very well send Christmas cards if I don't know the return address. Maybe I'm on the corner."

A splintered pony cart caught his eye. One of the shells had exploded nearby and overturned it. He stared at it a moment and muttered, "Somehow I'd have imagined it more scenic."

The barn was still standing. Perhaps because there had been little wind and perhaps because the house and barn were a hundred yards apart, no spark had jumped the gap.

On the path from the house to the barn lay a hound, its chest blown open, innards spilling out.

A dead chicken lay nearby.

Nothing moved.

Just another casualty," the soldier said, picking up the dead chicken by its feet and holding it at arm's length, "in a long list of casualties. Some Christmas, all right. Not even a Christmas goose this year." He tossed the chicken carcass aside.

Something moved. Barn door. He dropped to the ground, finger on trigger, and waited for an enemy soldier to step out. He held his breath, his heart pounding fast and hard in his ears.

A kitten. A white kitten. As it pushed past the door, the hollow-eyed soldier felt his muscles relax and his breath rush out.

"No," he whispered, tensing again. "Could still be someone inside." His finger tightened on the trigger again as he thought what to do.

It was dusk. He had been separated from his outfit. It was Christmas Eve in a war zone, he was bone-tired, and he wasn't even sure what country he was in. He needed a place to sleep, and it was either the barn or the woods. But he wasn't sure the barn was empty.

When nothing moved for five minutes, he changed his position, working around to the back of the barn. Didn't trust the front. Too risky. Behind the barn he discovered a fenced stock pen with a low door leading inside. He entered cautiously, rifle barrel first.

The barn was dark, empty. The animals had either escaped, been eaten or—like the hound and the chicken—been killed in the shelling. The stalls were empty except for the loose straw scattered for bedding. No hay. The Allied advance had turned the hay fields into battlefields.

The soldier looked into the rafters. Two identical lofts, one on each end of the barn.

"Heck of a Christmas Eve," he repeated under his

breath, then climbed the ladder to one of the lofts. Once up, he moved to a corner and pulled off his pack.

"Where's Santa with my presents tonight?" he said sarcastically. "I guess he and God stay clear of the combat zone."

He sat dazed a moment, stunned by the possibility of what he had uttered. This war and what he had seen and experienced had presented him with his times of most faith and least faith. Finally he took off his helmet, set it aside, and began pulling things from his pack.

A can of beans. Powdered milk. Two chocolate bars. The beautiful knitted shawl he had bought in a French village, hoping to send it home to his mother in Maine. In truth, though, he didn't want to send it; he preferred to hold onto it, praying that he might get home alive to place it around her neck himself.

He opened the beans and ate them along with one of the chocolate bars, then lay on the loose straw and fell asleep.

A noise woke him and his eyes flew open. Cautiously, silently, he sat up, rifle ready. No idea how long he'd slept. Not sure if it was night or day. A dim light. Was it dawn? After a moment his eyes adjusted and he saw that it was lantern light. He inched to the edge of the loft to peer down.

A young woman, hardly more than a child herself, sat on a bed of straw, nursing a baby. The child cooed as it sucked, and the mother sang a lullaby. No father or traveling companion in sight.

The hollow-eyed soldier kept silent.

3

After awhile the young mother lay back on the straw and lifted the child above her head.

The baby gurgled and giggled each time she lowered it to her face and kissed its belly. Once she held it overhead and it drooled on her, but she simply laughed and kept on. She sat up and kissed its bottom, then lay the baby across her lap and stroked its back and hair. The child flailed its arms and legs without crying, but didn't fall asleep.

When the baby tried to turn over and look up, the young mother stood, placing one hand behind the baby's head and another under its bottom. Then the two of them began to dance, swirling and dipping around the dirt floor together. The mother's long skirt kicked up tiny straw and dust whirlwinds, and the white kitten swiped at her with its paw.

The breathless young mother slowed to a waltz, and within minutes the baby fell asleep. She walked to one of the horse stalls, spread a white linen napkin on the straw, and laid the sleeping baby on it. Then she covered it with a second linen napkin, bowed her head, and silently prayed.

Another movement. From the other loft.

The soldier's hollow eyes searched the darkness there and met another pair of hollow eyes. The enemy. Each had been intent on the mother and child. Now they were intent on each other. For a long time neither moved, neither raised a weapon. Then, as if by design, both looked down again on the mother bowed over her sleeping child.

The enemy moved first, and the hollow-eyed soldier watched as his counterpart cautiously slung the rifle over his shoulder and began the climb down from the loft.

The sound of boots on the ladder startled the mother, and she looked up, afraid. But when the soldier smiled and nodded respectfully, she relaxed and acknowledged his nod. He knelt near her, reached a hand into his pack, and drew out a carved wooden box. When he lifted its lid, a waltz began.

The mother smiled as he held out the music box to her. Not a word spoken, and after a long moment the enemy soldier stood, slipped on his pack again, and disappeared into the night.

In the loft the hollow-eyed soldier waited to see if his enemy would return. When nothing happened after ten minutes, he swung his feet onto the ladder and climbed down quietly while the young mother watched. As his boots touched the floor he turned and faced her, unsure what to do next. His tentativeness gave way and he slipped off his pack to kneel where his enemy had knelt. One hand held the pack and the other slid inside it, drawing out the powdered milk and the remaining candy bar. He placed them beside his enemy's music box.

The mother nodded, smiled, and the soldier rose to leave. But at the door he stopped. He looked back to the light, seemed uncertain for a moment, then retraced his steps and knelt once more where his enemy had knelt.

The music box had run down, the waltz had stopped. He picked it up, turned it over in his calloused hands. Solid yet delicate, the work of a master, he could see. The music box was indeed a fine gift.

He wound it, opened the lid, and the waltz began anew.

The mother smiled, and when she saw the hollow-eyed soldier looking down toward her sleeping infant, she drew back the linen napkin to reveal its peaceful face. Tears streamed down the soldier's cheeks.

The young mother bowed her head, eyes closing softly. As she did, he closed his eyes and bowed his head. It was only a moment, a long moment in the midst of a long war, but when she looked up, the hollow-eyed soldier was gone. And where he had knelt sat the music box playing its waltz. Draped across its open lid lay a beautiful knitted shawl.

6

The Magi's Gift

Matthew looked at the clock for the umpteenth time. Six-fifteen. Only a little over an hour until pageant time. Gram Bryant had said he could leave at six-thirty. Matthew was itching to go.

One year he'd played Joseph, Jesus' father. Another year he'd played an angel, with a coat hanger halo that kept bouncing and hitting him on the forehead, and tin foil wings that were forever brushing against the piano or against the church flag in the small chancel area.

In kindergarten he'd played a donkey, which was a step up from the previous year when he'd been a sheep, and when he was a first-grader he played a shepherd.

His mother had been alive then, and she and Gram had never tired of telling how Matthew and his cousin Freddy (also a shepherd) nearly poked out the Dennis sisters' eyes by nervously wobbling and tapping their shepherds' crooks. The two honey-voiced teens had gotten to laughing so hysterically they couldn't finish their duet. Matthew thought that he remembered it, but he wasn't really sure, because it could be that it was simply the retellings he was recalling.

This year would be his first chance to try a new part, a Magi, one of the three wise kings from the East. Matthew was excited, because the Magi were the best-dressed in the cast (if you didn't count angels as being well-dressed, which he didn't), and the Magi got to deliver gifts. The robes were surely better than Mary's and Joseph's clothing, and much sharper looking than the dusty shepherd garb. Besides, Gram had bought him a nice gold terrycloth bathrobe for the occasion, one with his initials—MPW—monogrammed on the breast. The robe would look like a true king's finery and, after its pageant duty, would be nice and warm on Maine's coldest winter nights.

"Here's the candle, Matthew," Gram said, handing him a candle the size of a coffee can. "Don't forget to say your mother's name when you light it from the altar candle."

The candle was a blend of many colors. No mistake that it was the size and shape of a coffee can, because throughout the year Matthew and his grandmother had saved the stubs from dozens of different colored candles and melted them together to make one great rainbow candle. The church's tradition was to include a brief time at the end of the Nativity Pageant when parishioners could light candles they'd brought along in memory of loved ones, then place them around the manger area.

Last year had been the first time Matthew and Gram had made a rainbow candle to light in memory of Matthew's mother Carol, Gram's daughter. Gram called it "a candle of hope, like the rainbow Noah saw from the ark." They'd lit it together then, but this year, with Gram wheelchair-bound from a broken hip she suffered in a Thanksgiving fall, Matthew was going to church alone to light the candle for both of them.

"It smells good, Gram," Matthew said, holding the candle under his nose.

"It's that cinnamon we put in," she said. "I told you it would give a lovely fragrance. It's how your Mom and I used to scent the candles we made when she was your age."

Matthew smiled, trying to imagine his mother being his age.

The hallway clock struck once. Six-thirty. Time to go.

Matthew opened the door.

"Got everything?" Gram asked, offering a check list like in the morning when Matthew headed off to school.

"Bathrobe?"

"Check."

"Candle?"

"Check."

"Cookies?"

"Che—" Matthew stopped mid-word. He'd forgotten the tollhouse cookies Gram had baked especially for Reverend Tyler. Matthew and Gram both liked him a lot. He had conducted Matthew's mother's funeral. Tollhouse cookies were his favorite.

The cookies were still on the kitchen table, wrapped in aluminum foil and nestled inside a beautifully decorated maroon and silver fruitcake tin. Matthew was to give the cookies to Reverend Tyler as

9

a Christmas gift right away, then use the expensive-looking container as his Magi prop for the Nativity Pageant. He would bend with a noble bow and leave the maroon and silver tin at the feet of the Christ child, his kingly gift.

Matthew returned to the front hallway pretending to be out of breath from his mad dash to the kitchen for the cookies.

"Check!" he said with a broad grin on his face, cookie tin in front of him. Bathrobe. Candle. Cookies."

He worked the thick candle into his coat pocket, folded the bathrobe and slid it into a rope-handled shopping bag, and placed the cookie tin in the bag on top of the bathrobe. He kissed his grandmother and walked out the door as she waved goodbye from her wheelchair.

"And don't dawdle, Matthew," she called. "You go straight to church."

Gram Bryant knew his inclinations. Matthew was a lot like his mother had been.

The evening air was chilly and the light breeze bit into Matthew's skin. A few large, clean snowflakes drifted lazily downward, seeming to come from the street lights above.

One landed on Matthew's nose. He stuck out his tongue to catch the coldness of another, and its feel on his tongue reminded him of the night his mother had taken him sledding on Puckerbrush Hill. They'd set three kerosene lanterns at the top of the hill, halfway down, and at the bottom to light their sled run, and then he'd sat with his mother behind him, her legs and arms wrapped around him, cutting through the crisp air again and again, until finally they were exhausted from the climbs back up Puckerbrush Hill and they had to trudge home and warm up with hot chocolate with marshmallows in it.

Matthew passed the cedar-shingled blacksmith shop that was falling down. It was a small barn more than a hundred years old and hadn't been used as a blacksmith shop, folks said, for twenty years. Its roof leaked and had begun to cave in at the back.

Most of the windows were broken out. But no one would think of tearing it down, because the old blacksmith was ninety-five and in a nursing home. But no one wanted to be a blacksmith and use it, and no one had the authority to tear it down, so it was gradually collapsing onto itself.

Matthew noticed a rough pine wreath on the heavy barn door. Through a broken window pane in the door he glimpsed a glow of light, and when he cupped his hands around his eyes and peered inside, he saw a man warming his hands over a small bed of coals in the old blacksmith's forge.

The man hummed something, but Matthew couldn't make out the tune or the words. Maybe a Christmas carol?

"Merry Christmas," the man said, as if he had eyes in the back of his head the way Gram did. He kept his hands spread over the coals, fingers spread the same way Matthew's mother held her hands when she was drying her nail polish.

"Merry Christmas," Matthew answered. "Whatcha doin'?"

"Keepin' warm."

"In the blacksmith shop?"

"Yup. I live here sometimes."

"Why?"

"Gotta live somewhere."

Now Matthew recognized him. He was the odd-jobs man everyone called Dusty. Matthew didn't know his real name, but he did remember Gram hiring him to rake the leaves in the yard a few times. And he'd painted the fence. Some of the kids were scared of him and called him Cyclops, because he had only one good eye, the bad one being a dead, milky color.

"You're Dusty, right?"

"Yup. And yourself?"

"Matthew Wallace. You painted my Gram Bryant's fence."

The man had on two flannel shirts, Matthew noticed, the collar showing the inner one to be solid green, the outer one being red-and-white checked. Behind him in a corner, lit by a flickering candle in a saucer, was a cot piled high with blankets.

"Musta been two summers ago I painted that fence," Dusty said. "How's it holdin' up?"

"Good."

"That's good," Dusty said. "And was that you watching me from the porch then?"

"That was me."

Matthew could see, even in the dim light, that Dusty's eyebrows were thick and almost connected at the outer edges to his wild beard. He wore a Russian Cossack hat on his head.

"You've grown since then," Dusty said.

"Yeah," Matthew said, and the two of them remained silent a moment.

"Must be it was your mother who died then? Sometime that fall after I painted the fence."

"Yeah," Matthew said again, faintly. "She was sick more than a year."

"Sorry to hear it," Dusty answered. "Must be hard for you."

"Yeah," Matthew said. "It is."

Another silence.

"Cold enough for ya out there?" Dusty finally said.

"Oh, you bet," Matthew answered, still not stepping into the blacksmith shop. "Must be cold in here at night, huh?"

13

"Well, sometimes. Not too, too bad at the moment. I keep burning what's left of the old blacksmith's soft coal in the forge. Keeps the chill off. Can't complain."

"You make this wreath?" Matthew touched the circle of pine branches on barn door.

"Yup."

"It's nice."

Matthew worried a clump of the wreath's pine needles like a Rosary between his thumb and fingertips.

"I'm on my way to church, to the pageant," he said. "You going?" He knew the answer as the words left his tongue.

"Nah. I'm not much on church. Besides, fire'd go out."

"Yeah, I suppose," Matthew said. "Well, I gotta

go. I'm a king this year."

"Have a good time."

"I will. See ya, Mr. Dusty."

"Dusty. Call me Dusty, son."

"Okay. See ya, Dusty."

"Bye, Matthew."

Matthew started away, then after two or three steps turned back and called through the broken window, "Would you like some Christmas cookies, Dusty? Tollhouse. My grandmother made 'em."

Before the man could answer, Matthew had set his shopping bag down by the door and removed the maroon and silver cookie tin from where it rested on the folded gold bathrobe. He stepped inside, popping the lid from the tin as he went, and withdrew Reverend Tyler's packet of foil-wrapped tollhouse cookies.

"Here," he said, presenting the cookies.

Dusty slid his hands under the packet, his fingers brushing the boy's as he accepted it.

Matthew felt the heat of Dusty's coal-warmed hands.

"Thanks," Dusty said, a smile revealing laugh lines under both the good eye and the milky eye.

"You're welcome," Matthew said.

The candle by the cot flickered, and Dusty cast a backward glance at it. All that remained in the saucer was a shimmering pool of wax and the fluttering end of a wick.

"The draft," Matthew said. "I'd better close the door."

As he turned to leave, the heavy candle in his

pocket clunked against his hip. He slid his hand into his pocket to steady it.

"Awful glad you came, Matthew," Dusty said.

Matthew looked back at this man in the two flannel shirts and Russian hat who stood by the glowing forge with a bundle of foil-wrapped cookies glinting and twinkling on his palms. Matthew thought Dusty looked oddly like a king just then, a Magi bearing a gift.

Matthew's hand curled around the warm, soft candle in his pocket. He could feel his fingers making an impression on the wax.

"Would a bathrobe help you keep warm?" Matthew asked, not knowing what else to say. His eyes searched Dusty's face. "I've got one here, you know, in the bag."

15

"I've got clothes aplenty," Dusty said with a playful grin and a twinkle in his good eye. "As you can see, I've got so many shirts I have to wear two at a time. And I've got loads of blankets."

The candle flickered again, but didn't go out.

Matthew gazed downward at nothing in particular, his hand gripping the candle in his pocket tight. He walked back to the door and pushed it open again, then caught up the rope grip of the shopping bag with his free hand.

"Gotta go," he mumbled, and started off in the direction of the church.

But before he had traveled a dozen steps, he spun on his heel and trotted back to the blacksmith shop, where he knocked on the heavy door.

"Dusty?" he called.

"Come in," a muffled voice inside answered.

Matthew stepped in and found Dusty sitting on the edge of his cot, mouth already stuffed with tollhouse cookies.

The man in the Cossack hat grinned up at Matthew as the boy marched across the firelit room, one hand toting a shopping bag, the other hand drawing something out of his coat pocket.

"Dusty, here's one that won't burn out for a long, long time," Matthew said, and he handed the man his mother's coffee-can-sized rainbow candle. "Merry Christmas."

Dusty, mouth still stuffed with cookies, mumbled "Merry Chriff-muff" as Matthew turned and walked out into the night, where huge snowflakes floated down from street light halos to land on the boy's head and sometimes on the tip of his tongue.

The Blessing Bell

They called it the Blessing Bell, the heavy cast-iron bell in the steeple of St. Mary's Church. It wasn't the regular bell, not the small, more modern one used from week to week. No, this was the Blessing Bell, the historic original bell, and it got used only once a year, on Christmas Eve. For a hundred and fifty years, from 1809 until now—1959—every December 24th at midnight this bell had poured out the blessings of the Virgin and her Christ child on this fishing village, one of only several on the Maine coast that claimed to be home to so many Catholics. In those hundred and fifty years very few fishermen had perished at sea, and the village had been faithful and cared well for the families of those lost there. Now, in less than a week, the bell would bless the village and its people once again.

Patrick was very excited, for he was one of the altar boys at St. Mary's Church on the square, and this was his year to pull the bell rope twelve times at midnight to bless the village.

He was eleven, as was his brother James, the twin who'd had the bad luck to be born fourteen minutes later. Bad luck for James because the honor of yanking the Christmas rope, as some referred to it, always fell to the eldest of the altar boys still under the age of twelve, even if Patrick was the elder by only fourteen minutes. Whichever brother got to do it, though, Patrick or James, it was a great honor for the family.

The problem for James was that he wouldn't be able to yank the Christmas rope the following year either, because he'd be over twelve years old and ineligible. So the only way James would ever bless the village was if, God forbid, something happened to Patrick so he couldn't do it this year.

Patrick's and James's father had himself rung the Blessing Bell twenty-five years earlier, as a ten year-old altar boy. And their grandfather had rung it thirty years before that, when he was nine. The twins' older brother Joseph had rung it as well, three years ago, having squeaked under the wire by being eleven years and three hundred sixty days on Christmas Eve.

Patrick could hardly sleep nights for the anticipation of it. He pictured himself standing in the narthex of the church, making that first yank on the huge braided rope that disappeared up out of sight through a hole cut in the ceiling. Every Sunday after mass he would pass that bell rope and think of *Jack and the Beanstalk*, imagining himself shinnying up it to a grand kingdom in the clouds.

This year, on Christmas Eve, Patrick would jump up, put all his weight on that rope and wait for the delay, that seemingly endless moment when came no sound—something his brother Joseph had warned him about—but then, in time, the Blessing Bell would peal out its magnificent note across the crisp night air. Patrick would pull it again and again, eleven more times, pull it with all the joy and purpose he had heard his brother and father and grandfather speak of. And the village would be blessed, the sailors safe.

But two days before Christmas, Patrick couldn't rise from his bed. A fever gripped him and he could barely breathe. The doctor stopped by several times, as did the priest, Father Callahan. When chills set in, Patrick's grandmother and mother took turns at his bedside, piling the extra blankets on and spooning soup into him.

The doctor called it pneumonia and said it was extremely serious. No, he said, Patrick would not be able to ring the Blessing Bell. He would need all his strength and energies just to survive, and for healing.

Patrick felt devastated. He had waited so long for this Christmas Eve, for the moment he could pull the bell rope and bless his village.

Once, when Patrick's mother and the doctor thought he was asleep, he saw the two of them standing by his door, whispering. The doctor shook his head sadly and said, "All we can do now is wait, and pray for him."

In his feverish nightmares Patrick saw the bell rope. But in the dreams he couldn't grasp it, for it was always just out of his reach. Or, if he managed to clutch the knot in the rope's end, he would find he was too weak to pull the cord properly. Or sometimes in the dream, he pulled the cord but no sound came out, only silence.

On Christmas Eve morning James came into the bedroom to check on his brother, who seemed to him weaker than the previous day. From his sickbed

19

Patrick seemed to sense it too, and he insisted on giving James instructions on how to ring the bell in his stead. James thought that what Patrick really seemed to be doing was passing on a blessing.

After he left the bedroom, James stood outside the door, overhearing his brother's prayer: "Holy Father, bless my brother James tonight, and help me be beside him in spirit."

James said his own prayer, asking forgiveness in case he had in some way wished this illness upon his brother so that he might take Patrick's place at the bell rope.

Snow began to fall at dusk and several inches covered the ground by the time the tower clock ticked its last few minutes toward midnight. From his bedroom window Patrick could see the steeple of St. Mary's across the village square. The light atop the bell tower shone bright, reminding him of the star over Bethlehem on that first Christmas Eve. He knew James would ring the Blessing Bell well, and when he pictured his twin brother pulling on the rope, it wasn't hard to picture himself doing it. Patrick blinked back tears as he waited for the sound of the bell.

Suddenly he heard a commotion on the staircase, then in the hallway outside his room. James burst in, accompanied by several other boys who remained close to the door. In his hands he held a length of rope with a knot in it. It looked like the bell rope, except this rope ran out the door into the hallway. The other altar boys held onto the same rope at intervals, so James and they together looked like volunteer firemen dragging a hose into a burning building.

Patrick stared in puzzlement.

"It's almost midnight," James said. "The Blessing Bell, Patrick. Are you ready?"

He laid the hank of rope across the bedcovers, giving over the knotted end to his sick brother.

Patrick grasped it.

"It's too long," he protested weakly. "If it's connected to the bell, that's a great distance. It will be too heavy to pull." A look of dismay came over Patrick's face, as if a cruel joke were being played on him.

"It's connected, Patrick," James said. "But not in the usual way. Look out there."

Patrick peered out toward St. Mary's Church. In the falling snow stood a chain of people—men, women, children; friends, neighbors, relatives— linked together hand in hand, stretching across the square from the church to the house, up into his bedroom. From his bed they looked like a chain of cutout paper angels.

"Hurry, Patrick," James said. "It's midnight. The Blessing Bell. The time to bless the people has come."

Indeed it had. Patrick could see Father Callahan across the square on the church steps, waving his arms. Then he dropped his hand as a signal.

Patrick, weak and still weighed down by the blankets, started to protest to his brother, "But you—"

But then he saw the urgency in his brother's face and he braced his feet against the footboard of the bed and, as if pulling an anchor free of a muddy sea bottom, yanked the Christmas rope with all his strength.

The rope moved.

But no sound followed. This was far longer than the delay Joseph had spoken of.

Patrick stared out the window onto the square. Then he saw movement, a ripple in the line of connected people. First one person, then the next, then the next. There was no physical rope connecting them, only hands linked to hands. It was like watching a slow fuse burn, but after a long minute, finally there came the low sweet note of the Blessing Bell showering its Good News out into the night air over the village.

Patrick pulled—two, three, four, up to twelve—and the blessings poured forth again and again until his brother James hugged him and Patrick lay back on his pillow, smiling, exhausted.

It's hard to say who was most blessed that Christmas Eve in 1959—Patrick, James, or the villagers. But Patrick's fever did break that night, and he ate the Christmas meal with his family the next day.

In 1989 Patrick's son rang the Blessing Bell. And in 1991 (times change) it was his twin brother James's daughter who yanked the Christmas rope.

The village continues to be blessed.

The Thumb Island Elephants

My name is Elvira Whipple and I've lived on the Thumb my whole life. I'm ninety-four and not real healthy, so I thought I'd tell why the Congregational Church manger scene has more than the usual Biblical animals in it; this one has two papier-mache elephants.

Christmas Eve 1909 I was a week shy of turning ten. It snowed all day, so we had a foot of new snow atop a foot of old. My father was a deacon at Thumb Island Congregational Church and my mother sang in the choir. I was so eager to get to the eight o'clock service of hymns and candles I could hardly eat supper.

As most folks know, Thumb Island (or the Thumb, as most people call it) isn't an island at all. It's a village that occupies a small peninsula, water on its south, east, and west, and it juts into Fisher's Island Sound like a swelled thumb. The coastal railway crosses it at the north end where it connects to the mainland, so it looks on a map as if a thumb's been lopped off and stitched back on. As far back as I can remember, locals have simply called it the Thumb.

Back when I was growing up we had five churches on the Thumb: Congregational, Baptist, Episcopal, Roman Catholic, and Shiloh. I never really understood the differences, and I can see now that much of what I learned was incorrect. What I thought my parents and other adults were saying was this:

The Episcopalians were kissing cousins to the Church of England. You didn't have to be wealthy to belong, but it helped, and it helped if you could trace your lineage. My father said they made too much of a show of their religion when they worshiped. (I later learned that they were very *liturgical*.)

The Baptists were similar to us Congregationalists except they dunked people to baptize them. We sprinkled ours. Baptist prayers were longer, too.

The Catholics were people we were supposed to avoid. Many were from Europe—fishermen and their families who didn't speak good English, my parents said. They made the sign of the cross when they passed their own church. On the other hand, Episcopalians, Baptists, and Congregationalists made a point of crossing the street to avoid meeting the Catholic priest. For reasons I did not understand, Catholicism was the farthest thing from Protestantism. Still, we bought fish from the Catholics, and to me it tasted the same as Protestant-caught fish.

I don't know if Shiloh was a black Baptist or a black Methodist church, but it was near the railroad tracks. Its members were mostly the families of railroad porters or ships' stewards. Some folks called it Shiloh Church, but most said "the colored church." I had no idea what Shilohs believed, but I loved to go by their church in summer when the doors and windows were open, so I could listen to them singing. If there was anything like an Ecumenical Movement back in 1909, it never got across the tracks from the mainland and onto the Thumb.

I thought we'd never leave for church that Christmas Eve, but finally we did. We walked through the deep snow and I arrived out of breath. My mother went to the balcony to join the choir, and my father walked to the pulpit to talk with the minister about communion.

Mr. Moody's organ prelude filled the church. I sat back and inhaled the smells of the church as if they were my lifeblood—the slight mustiness, the polished pews, the candles, the heat from the downstairs wood furnace rising up through the floor registers. When I opened my eyes and looked behind me at the clock hung from the back balcony, it said one minute before eight. The organ prelude ended and the congregation hushed for the opening anthem.

A loud voice shattered the silence.

"Friends! We need your help."

I spun around and looked back toward the doors that led from the foyer into the sanctuary. Directly under the clock stood a black man in a suit, his hands stretched in front of him as if he were preparing to direct a choir. I recognized him as one of the railroad porters.

No one moved.

"A wagon's stuck on the tracks. We can't get it off."

We all stared at him. This was the first time any

black person had ever set foot in our church.

"Please," he pleaded. "It's a big circus wagon."

The church emptied, everyone following him to the grade crossing. There were no passenger trains on Christmas Eve, but there might be a freight. Most nights we could count on one around eleven-thirty.

At the grade crossing we found a huge wagon, like one I'd seen for transporting prisoners, tipped over on its side. This one, though, was bright red with gold trim. It was longer than two stagecoaches and built like a small railroad boxcar, and across its ends it said Barnum & Bailey, the Greatest Show on Earth. The wagon had small slits for windows on either end. A man stood at one of the windows, talking into it, cooing softly the way you'd calm a baby. A team of four brown-and-white draft horses stood there, still hitched.

Four or five black men held lanterns. The Shilohs had arrived first, since their church was only a hundred yards from the crossing.

After a minute or two, two small crowds arrived, Episcopalians and Baptists, led by a different black man from Shiloh. Right behind the black man was the Baptist minister in his white shirt, black suit, and overcoat, followed by the Episcopal rector who still had his black robe on, which showed beneath his coat.

I could tell from the way the snow was tramped down and from the sweat on their faces that the Shiloh people had been struggling awhile with the wagon.

"What happened?" my father asked, and the man

who had been cooing into the wagon stepped toward him.

"I was driving this team from Boston to New York City for Barnum and Bailey, but the storm caught me. The horses were worn out, so I headed for Thumb Island. I hit the tracks a little off square and when the wagon tilted, the elephants must've shifted their weight inside so the wagon tipped."

"Elephants?" my father said.

As the adults talked I sneaked up to the wagon's slitted window. A black girl named Hannah, about my age, stood beside me with a lantern and we peered in.

I had never seen an elephant before, only pictures. The mother lay on her side, and the flank which showed looked dusty. It rose and fell like a swelling sea. Her head was massive, and under it I could see a crumpled ear as big as my coat if I spread it on the ground.

"Look at that eye," Hannah said. "It's beautiful, like a cow eye."

What she said was true. The huge eye had the same foolish, gentle look as a cow staring over a fence, waiting to be handed a handful of grass.

The baby elephant stayed by its mother, not nursing, just standing. They stared up at us and the mother seemed to sigh. I expected the smell of manure to drift out the barred window, but what I breathed in was more the scent of a baby after a bath, a fresh-bread smell. I wanted to touch them, to learn what their hide felt like, to see if it felt the way our school-teacher, Miss Harms, said an elephant's hide felt, not rough and dry, but soft and silky.

"Hey, look," someone said, and Hannah and I stepped back. There came the Catholics, their young, handsome, newly arrived black-haired priest in his robes leading the procession.

"What's wrong?" he asked.

"Two elephants in the wagon," my father said.

"And we can't get them out?" the priest answered.

"The doors are on either side of the wagon," the driver said. "So one's down against the track and the other faces straight up."

"Can't we tip it back up?" the priest asked.

"No," the wagon driver said, shaking his head. "A bunch of us tried. But it's not just the weight of the wagon. You've got a five ton elephant plus the baby. Every time we try to right it, the elephants get nervous and shift their weight, forcing us back down."

"How about getting them out first, then moving it?" our church's minister said.

The Episcopal rector thought that was a good idea, and suggested chopping a hole and removing one entire end of the wagon. But the wagon driver reminded us the wagon had been reinforced with iron bars.

"After all," he said. "It's designed to hold elephants."

The mother trumpeted, and we all jumped back.

"Excuse me," said the black man who had burst into our church. "The land is flat here at the grade crossing, which is why we're always trying to lift the wagon up. But what if we skid the wagon along on top of the tracks—like hauling a boat? Look. It's only two hundred yards to the cove beach where the track runs on top of that rock pile. The beach is lower than the track, so we can tip the wagon *down* instead of *up*. It'd be a lot easier."

Everyone stared at the man, then looked to the wagon driver who shrugged his shoulders.

"Worth a try," the driver said. "But the snow's pretty deep, and we'll need a wider path than a train."

He pointed at the foot of new snow that had accumulated on the track and then at the two feet of old and new snow alongside it.

"We'll have to clear it," the priest said flatly. He made a megaphone with his hands and announced, "Friends, we must clear a wide path to the beach so we can drag the wagon there. Hurry."

29

In no time we had a hundred or more people, all carrying shovels, ropes, and chains. Two oxen appeared along with some horses. By ten-fifteen we had a wide path cleared to the cove and the oxen and horses had been hooked up. Folks tied on more ropes and every person there grabbed on like it was a tug-of-war at the County Fair.

And we pulled, all of us. My Lord, did we pull. The wagon came by inches and feet, slow because we had to keep changing positions. Hannah and I pulled at first, until my father gave us each a lantern and told us to stand on the rock trestle in case we had to signal an approaching freight train coming from Mystic with a snowplow on its nose. Two other girls took lanterns down the track to the east and stood watch there.

Hannah's and my teeth chattered as we stood on

that rock trestle that had been built to get a train across the tidal cove. While we shivered, everyone else heaved and sweated. We could see them wiping their foreheads with their sleeves.

After we'd been out there awhile, Hannah said, "Vira, you think we'll beat the train?"

"God only knows," I said, which felt true.

We gazed down the tracks toward the wagon. The piled-up snow on either side of the tracks made it look like a tunnel with no roof. Dozens and dozens of lanterns sat like luminaria atop the banked white snow, lighting the way, lovelier than any Christmas candlelight service I've seen since.

Down along the track, groaning and sweating, inching the wagon toward us to save those lovely, lovely elephants, we could see black folks and white folks, horses and oxen, Catholics and Protestants, the sprinkled and the dunked, all working side by side. Lordy, I thought, what God wouldn't give to have me and Hannah's view. As soon as I thought it, I realized God was right there seeing it, an arm around each of us.

A little past eleven-thirty we finally got the wagon positioned on the track above the beach. The team drivers set up their horses and oxen on the south side of the tracks while anyone not handling animals went to the north. People were to pull until the wagon tipped and started sliding downhill, at which time the animals would pull the opposite way and serve as counterweights to slow the slide.

The plan worked perfectly. Almost. We pulled, the wagon shifted balance. Then zoot—it slid, yanking horses and oxen ten feet back. Ka-whump! The wagon crashed onto the frozen beach and all four wheels snapped like soda crackers. But the wagon stayed upright.

The terrified elephants trumpeted and banged against the wagon's walls. Then they were silent and we all hushed. I looked down. Hannah was clutching my hand.

"Lord, bless these elephants," she whispered.

"Amen," I said.

The wagon driver held up a lantern and peered in.

"They're okay," he said.

We all cheered, and people began shaking hands and hugging, forgetting they were white and black, Catholic and Protestant. You'd have thought a home-town boy had just won a big race or a war had ended. Some people sat in the snow and wept. I don't know if the tears had to do with elephants or exhaustion or both, or if they were about seeing folks together like that.

Then a familiar voice yelled, "It's Christmas Day!"

It was my father, holding up his pocket watch up and pointing at it. A minute after midnight. I never saw him so excited.

Someone started in with *O Come, All Ye Faithful*, and before long everyone was singing. That's what we were doing five minutes later when the freight roared through—we were all singing Christmas carols and smiling. The engineer, seeing what looked like a tunnel of lights, must have thought this was a Christmas celebration for him. He cut his speed in half, waved

31

and grinned and yelled Merry Christmas from his cab like Santa Claus from his sleigh as the noisy locomotive severed the Thumb on its way east.

During the night the driver moved the elephants to a horse shed behind Shiloh Church, where people came by to visit them all Christmas day. It was strange to see folks from everywhere lined up at the Shiloh Church to catch a glimpse of the Thumb Island Elephants.

And they did feel smooth and silky, Hannah and I found out.

The day after Christmas a replacement wagon showed up, and the elephants set off again on their journey.

So there's the story and there's your answer. Now you know why the Thumb's Congregational Church manger scene has two gray papier-mache elephants that are about eighty-five years old.

I made the dark-skinned one and my lifelong best friend Hannah made the light-skinned one.

Or maybe it was the other way around. Doesn't matter, really.

Christmas Mouse

Friedrich the German mouse was feeling lonely. It was Christmas Eve and he was the only mouse left aboard the German freighter which lay anchored in Bombay Harbor. All the other mice had gone ashore for the holidays. As he looked across the darkened harbor at the twinkling lights of the other ships in port, Friedrich remembered the Christmases he had spent in Berlin with his widowed sister Frieda and her mouslings. He recalled the joy he felt as he watched them open their presents and empty their stockings. What satisfaction it had given him to make sure there were small treasures and fruits among their gifts!

As Friedrich peered up into the December sky over India, he saw a bright star, the brightest he had ever seen in that part of the world. It seemed to wink at him, and as it did, he envisioned the porcelain figures of Frieda's nativity scene on her fireplace. The red and green lights on the ships' masts reminded him of Christmas trees. Friedrich wondered how many other mice were alone and far from home and their families this Christmas Eve.

Friedrich's loneliness finally got the better of him, and he began to squeak loudly at the French tanker off to starboard. There was an answering squeak, but it was in French, and Friedrich the German mouse didn't squeak French. The mouse who answered apparently couldn't squeak German, so the conversation stopped there.

Friedrich spotted an American ship to port and squeaked his Christmas greetings again across the dark harbor. This time the answer was in English, but Friedrich didn't squeak English either, so the conversation stopped.

Friedrich the German mouse felt trapped on an island in a sea of loneliness far from home. He began to cry, and as he cried he felt the loneliness of Mary and Joseph on the night Jesus was born—turned out of the inn at Bethlehem, lucky to even find a stable in which to stay the night.

A Christmas carol came to mind—*Stille Nacht (Silent Night)*. It felt so right that Friedrich began to sing it softly as he stared at the silhouettes of ships on the starlit waters. By the end of the first verse the night air was filled with the sound of voices singing, each in his or her own language, *Silent Night, Holy Night*. The harbor was alive with the beauteous music of the heavenly host, and amid the spirit and joy of that moment on Christmas Eve, Friedrich the German mouse found his loneliness easier to bear.

Perfect, Just Perfect

It was four days before Christmas, and no sign of snow in the air. Everything in town lay still, as if Old Man Winter had forgotten the snow everyone was wishing for. Grampa and I were working at the department store. He was Santa Claus and I was his helper. He did the ho-hoing and asked kids what they wanted for Christmas. I was the candy-cane-and-present-passer-outer. Our hours were from four until seven-thirty.

Grampa's beard was real. Some of the kids who tugged it were quite surprised. It wasn't pure white, but it was bushy and full. When Grampa ho-hoed, his stomach shook. He was Santa Claus, no question.

Most of the lap-sitters were under ten. They were pretty much alike, asking for bikes, dolls, radios, and games.

But one little girl was different. Her mother brought her up, and Grampa hoisted her onto his lap. Her name was Tina. She was blind.

"What do you want for Christmas, Tina?" Grampa asked.

"Snow," she answered shyly.

Grampa smiled. His eyes twinkled. "We'll see what we can do about that. But how about something for you, yourself? Something special?"

Tina hesitated, then whispered something in Grandpa's ear. I couldn't hear her words, but I saw a smile creep over Grampa's face.

"Sure, Tina," was all he said.

He took her hands in his and placed them on his cheeks. His eyes closed and he sat there smiling as the girl began to sculpt his face with her fingers. She paused here and there to linger, paying close attention to every wrinkle and whisker. She seemed to be memorizing with her fingers the laugh lines under Grampa's eyes and at the corners of his mouth. She stroked his beard and rolled its wiry ringlets between her thumbs and forefingers. When she finished, she paused to rest her palms on Grampa's shoulders.

He opened his eyes. They were twinkling.

Suddenly her arms flew out, encircling Grampa's neck in a crushing hug.

"Oh, Santa," she cried. "You look just like I knew you. You're perfect, just perfect."

As Tina's mother lifted her down from his lap, Grampa turned his head toward me. He smiled, then blinked, and a tear rolled down his cheek.

That night when my grandmother came to pick us up, I watched her help Grampa shift over from the Santa chair into his wheelchair. As she was positioning his limp legs on the foot rests, she said, "So, Santa, how was your day?"

He looked up at me and pressed his lips together. Then he looked down at Gramma, cleared his throat, and said with a tiny smile, "Sweetheart, it was perfect. Just perfect."

Outside it began to snow.

A Christmas Dozen

Otis trudged along the icy Interstate, feeling about as down as he'd ever felt on a Christmas Eve. The north wind bit at his hide and the temperature was dropping like a brick now that the sun had gone down. With the drifting snow swirling around, it was hard for the old black Labrador to see.

Otis tried to imagine himself back in front of the Alleys' fireplace. For fourteen years he had spent Christmas Eve in his human family's living room while they decorated the tree and each of them opened one gift the night before Christmas. They always made sure he had a gift, too—a box of dog bones or a new collar or a rawhide chewy. One year they surprised him with a beanbag doggy bed from L.L. Bean. Another year the twins built a drafty dog house, but it never got used. Otis always slept with the family.

Now he found himself cold and hungry, dragging his arthritic old legs along a desolate northern stretch of the Maine Turnpike, trying to piece together what had happened. He ran over events again and again, praying things would magically change with a retelling.

The Alleys—six of them and Otis—had been driving from Kittery to Houlton to visit Todd, the married son. Most of the luggage and presents were strapped on the roof rack, and the space behind the back seat in the station wagon was just big enough to accommodate two suitcases and Otis on his L.L. Bean doggy bed.

Then came the blowout. Everyone had piled out. The spare was in a compartment under Otis, so out into the snow he went.

The twins, who were ten, hadn't seen a rest area since Bangor, and they were ready for one. So they got permission to step into the woods. Otis went with them. Somehow, in the confusion and the excitement of getting back on the road, the family drove off, leaving Otis standing dumbstruck on the side of the road. He waited two hours in the stinging wind, but when darkness set in, he started walking in the direction the car had gone.

After two or three hours and a close call with a snow plow, Otis came to a slight incline that led up to a rest area. It was a primitive one, no more than a roadside turn-out. No buildings, no rest rooms, no shelter from the wind and cold. It had been plowed— probably by the plow that had almost hit him—but already the drifting snow was covering the driver's work. There were no lights, and Otis thought it must be the darkest night of the year.

I'd even settle for that drafty dog house, he thought.

Then something in the snow caught his eye. A barrel. A sand barrel for people whose cars couldn't make the icy incline. It was no more than an old oil drum propped on its side with a half-moon slice cut from one end. The sand barrels were everywhere along the Maine roads in winter. The opening was tight, and Otis' arthritic hindquarters ached as he squeezed through, but he made it. Once inside, he curled up and fell asleep thinking about his family.

He awoke with a start, ears pricking up.

Silence.

Then he heard it again. A wailing. A pitiful wailing. Someone in pain. Otis worked his way around so he could look out into the darkness. It was so black and the snow swirled so furiously that he couldn't see his paw in front of his face.

"Who is it?" Otis called out. "Are you hurt?"

Only the wind.

Then a faint voice, very close by, said, "I'm freezing. I'm freezing, and I'm about to have my babies."

41

Otis peered out of the barrel into the darkness, but still he saw nothing—just blinding white against the black.

"Come inside," Otis said in his deep doggy voice. "Follow my voice." Silence again.

"I can't," the voice said finally. "You sound very big. And you might hurt me."

"I won't," the black Lab said. "Trust me, it's Christmas."

The word Christmas had barely left his mouth when a white face popped up at the opening of the sand barrel.

"You're a cat!" Otis exclaimed, deep voice rumbling all the more from inside the bowels of the barrel.

And indeed it was a cat, a delicate white cat with

a pink nose and black eyes, hardly more than a kitten herself. She was shivering.

The cat leaped back. "And you're a bear!" she exclaimed.

A standoff as they glared wide-eyed at each other.

"I am not a bear," Otis protested, his voice booming. Then he realized the cat couldn't see him in the shadowy blackness any better than he could see her in the swirling white. "I'm a dog," he continued in a softer voice. "I'll admit that I've got a little Newfoundland in me, and I may resemble a bear somewhat, but I am definitely a dog."

The cat began to shiver more violently and let out a long, agonizing meow. She was swollen and the time to deliver had come.

"Climb in," Otis said. "It's cramped, but it's out of the wind. And I'm warm. You can curl up with me."

So into the barrel she climbed, a bit cautious and nervous at first, but as her labor intensified she let go of her fear and curled up close to the warm old dog.

Through the long night the dog and the cat passed the time by sharing their stories.

Otis told her about the Alleys and how they had adopted him as a puppy. And Priscilla—for that was indeed the white cat's name—explained she had come from Florida with her mistress only a month before, so she had no winter coat. Her mistress found Maine too cold and decided to return to Florida. But she didn't want kittens, so she left Priscilla near a barn where there were other cats. The barn cats, however, were wild, and Priscilla was tame, and they treated her poorly, refusing to share their milk. Finally, lonely and hungry, Priscilla had left to follow the Maine Turnpike south. That was when the winter storm had hit and the time came for her kittens to be born.

By daybreak a blanket of snow covered the landscape and the rising sun began to warm the air. In the sand barrel, nestled between the old black Lab and the delicate white cat, lay twelve tiny pink-nosed kittens, eleven white ones and a gray one, taking turns nursing at their mother's breast.

"Aren't they beautiful?" Otis asked, his eyes dreamy. "A Christmas dozen."

But Priscilla looked distant, distracted.

"What's the matter?" Otis asked.

Silence. Then her eyes watered. "Where will we go?" she said sadly. "We have no home."

This time it was Otis who had no words. He thought for a minute, then said confidently, "Don't worry, you can share my family. And our fireplace."

Priscilla looked at Otis with doubt in her eyes.

"Do you really believe they'll come back?" she asked.

"Oh, they'll come," Otis assured her. "Don't worry. They'll come."

The two of them sat quietly for a minute, then two, then three. One kitten climbed over another's back.

"Are you sure?" Priscilla asked, looking up.

"Positive," Otis said. "Trust me, it's Christmas."

And they did come. Before midday the station wagon returned and the Alleys found him and hugged him and kissed him. And they took him home. And Priscilla. And her twelve kittens. Piled them all in the back of the station wagon with Otis on his L.L. Bean doggy bed. It was the warmest, brightest Christmas Otis could remember.

Christmas Prayers

rayers are funny things, aren't they? They may not always begin with Dear God or end with Amen. They may be spoken, at other times simply felt. Wishes and hopes, dreams and sighs, all sorts of yearnings, even absent-minded thoughts, apparently qualify as prayers. Indeed, prayers are funny things.

***

Father Jack Murphy and Pastor Tom Smith were more than colleagues in ministry in the tiny Eastern Long Island village, they were also friends, good friends, almost like brothers. And as sibling rivalry is wont to spring up unbidden between brothers, so too was there at times a mild rivalry between Jack and Tom that brought out their suppressed competitive sides. Usually it appeared within their common field—pastoral ministry—in comparisons of statistics (church stewardship, or mission giving, or membership figures, or church attendance).

But their competitive nature also showed up in the *personal* arena—particularly on the Holy Rollers bowling team they both belonged to at Mattituck

Lanes. Pastor Tom had never beaten Father Jack—not one single game in seven years together on the Rollers. A couple of times he'd come within a single pin of tying Jack (he'd even settle for a tie at first), but he'd never actually outscored him. Not that they were competing against each other—after all, they were on the same team. As naturally as dandelions materializing on a summer lawn, the rivalry just sprang up.

Even in this most joyous of seasons, Advent / Christmas, it was there.

Tom's small Methodist congregation was preparing for its traditional bathrobes-and-broomsticks Nativity Pageant in their sanctuary.

Jack's larger Roman Catholic congregation (without intending to compete) was pulling out all the stops and presenting a Live Nativity Scene outdoors in front of the church, complete with sheep, an ox, and a real baby boy born only two weeks earlier to the Logans.

Tom knew Jack hadn't meant for the two pageants to symbolize a competition, and they really didn't. Neither Jack nor Tom would allow such a thing to happen. But nevertheless it struck a competitive nerve in Tom, and he was jealous.

But pseudo-sibling rivalry or no, when Tom's wife Carol had suffered two miscarriages—Oh Lord, they longed for a child—it had been Father Jack Murphy who was there for them. When Tom broke his neck in a head-on collision after an Interfaith Council meeting one night, it was Jack whom Carol phoned from the hospital, and he came and stayed by Tom's bedside all night.

But it went both ways, and when Jack's father had died suddenly and unexpectedly in Boston, it was Pastor Tom Smith who drove his friend Jack to the funeral. They were very close, this East End village's Catholic priest and its Methodist minister, and they cared about each other like brothers.

Yet Tom couldn't help but think of the bowling, of his seven-year losing streak. And of Father Jack's Live Nativity Scene which would draw huge crowds— the Live Nativity Scene which, since it was later in the evening than the Methodist pageant, Tom had promised he and Carol would attend. They looked forward to seeing it, and they wanted to support their friend Jack. But still.

"I wish I could get one-up on Jack," Tom grumbled aloud one morning two days before Christmas. "Just once."

"Mmm," Carol said absently from her rocker by the woodstove. "Me, too."

On her lap rested several yards of fabric she was needlepointing, a runner for the communion table, her Christmas gift to the church. It would feature the new United Methodist logo that she and Tom loved, the cross and the flame.

Less than a mile away, Father Jack was hearing confessions. Millie Hampton, undoubtedly the poorest woman in town, sat bawling her eyes out on the other side of the confessional window. Widowed three years earlier and left penniless, she did tailoring and seamstress work at home. The Social Security check she received for herself and her daughter Megan wasn't much, and even when combined with her meager seamstress income she couldn't quite make ends meet. Now she had no money for Christmas dinner and stood in danger of losing her tiny house for three years of back taxes. Other than two store-bought toys, the only present she had to give little Megan was a Raggedy Ann doll she had made from yarn and fabric scraps.

"Here it is, Father," Millie said, choking back tears as she held the doll up to the confessional window. "Bless it, Father. Oh, please bless it."

Father Jack mumbled some words of blessing through the window. It wasn't the church's custom to pay delinquent tax bills, but a holiday meal for the less fortunate was in keeping with church policy. He made a mental note to himself to order a holiday meal for Millie and Megan—but perhaps because his mind was on the Live Nativity Scene, or on his recently deceased father in Boston, or on trying to properly bless a Raggedy Ann doll for which the church had no pat prayer—his mind misplaced the mental note.

* * *

I pray to God you two boys will straighten out," scolded Nancy Fellows. "I don't know what's gotten into you two lately."

Nancy's sons, eleven year-old Norman and ten year-old Nathan, stood looking shamefaced before her, their fingers and mouths smudged with chocolate.

"That cake was for supper," she continued. "Now upstairs to your bedroom. You can sit in suspense until your father gets home." The boys knew what would probably happen. They hadn't been spanked in a couple of years, but chocolate cake was their father's favorite, too. Upstairs they went, to mull over their situation.

That's when—stupid as the idea would sound later—they decided (two days before Christmas) to run away from home and become orange pickers in sunny Florida. They gathered what money they had in the bedroom, almost ten dollars, sneaked out the upstairs window onto the roof, and climbed down a tree to the snowy ground.

"Geez, it's awful cold," Nathan said, shivering as he pulled his jacket collar close around his neck. It had been ten to fifteen degrees below freezing every day for a week.

"We'll be okay once we hitch a ride in a warm car," Norman reassured him. "And the sun and beaches in Florida will be great."

***

Around the time Nancy Fellows was reprimanding her sons for pilfering her chocolate cake, Pastor Tom Smith and his wife Carol were deciding to drive to go scouting for stocking stuffers.

"I'll take my needlework," Carol said, holding up the table runner with the cross and flame for Tom to see.

"Gorgeous," he said. Then he winked and smiled and said, "So's the needlework."

Carol gave a mock scowl. "Come on," she said. "Let's go. Maybe I can find a white gift box to fit it."

But when they got into the car and buckled their seatbelts, the car's engine growled twice, three times, four times, and died.

"Forgot to hook up the battery charger last night," he said.

"Oh, well," Carol said with a shrug. "Put the charger on now and we'll hoof it to the Pharmacy. They've got stocking stuffers, too."

In no time the battery charger was connected and the Smiths were walking away, the table runner neatly folded on the front seat of the car.

***

Russell Preston, the retired high school superintendent, pulled into the driveway of the Methodist parsonage and saw the minister's car in front of the garage, its hood up, the battery charger's cables snaking over the grillwork. He shook his head.

"This poor guy hasn't had much luck lately," he mumbled. He pulled a frozen twelve-pound turkey from his shopping bag and carried it in his arms to the back door of the parsonage. He knocked and waited. No answer. Knocked again, waited. Tried the door. Locked.

What to do with the turkey? He had just bought it at the IGA, where the checkout cashier smiled and said, "Somebody's in for a big surprise this year." He'd thought she meant the lucky turkey buyer who would get the "Christmas Cash" promised on the window banners. But when she'd smiled and said it— "Somebody's in for a big surprise this year"—it reminded him of Pastor Tom his wife Carol, who could use a welcome surprise. Let it be them. And if they didn't need it, Tom might know where to direct the bird. Russell carried the frozen turkey to the disabled car, and placed it on the front seat.

***

"I'm freezing," Nathan Fellows whined. "We've been hitchhiking twenty minutes and nobody's stopped."

"Be patient," Norman said. "We're in the middle of the village. We can't hitchhike for awhile. Let's get past the Catholic Church and try again. Come on, we'll duck into this store for a minute and warm up."

After five minutes of "just looking" in the store, the boys were ready to resume their trek toward sunny Florida. They had walked along the sidewalk barely fifty yards when Norman grabbed Nathan and pulled him into the bushes beside the Methodist parsonage.

"I just saw Dad's car go by," Norman said. "I don't think he spotted us."

"Dad? You sure? He doesn't get home from work for hours," Nathan said.

"Maybe he took time off to Christmas shop. Let's work our way around behind these buildings," Norman said. "We can start in back of that garage and then go behind the church." The boys walked toward the parsonage garage and paused in front of the open-hooded car.

"Hey, look," Nathan said. "There's a turkey on the front seat."

Norman looked inside. "Yeah," he said. "A turkey. Good idea. We'll take it with us. We haven't got any other food. If we have to, we can find an empty summer cabin up on Laurel Lake or someplace and hole up for the night. Those places have fireplaces or woodstoves. We'll cook the turkey over an open fire like the Pilgrims did."

The idea made sense to Nathan. His older brother had thought of it, and it promised adventure.

"Grab it," Norman ordered, opening the passenger door. Nathan tugged on the frozen turkey.

"It's heavy," he said. "And slippery."

"Wrap that blanket around it, Nate," Norman said, indicating the folded table runner.

The Fellows Gang had struck and were now sneaking through back yards, taking turns lugging a small frozen turkey in a colorful blanket, escaping from frigid Eastern Long Island to the palmy, balmy beaches of Florida.

They got as far as the Catholic Church, where they stood on the curb, Norman's hitching thumb stuck out. Nathan cradled the bird in the blanket. It wasn't two minutes before Norman spotted a Town Police cruiser in the distance.

"Hide. It's the cops," he said.

"Hide where?" Nathan croaked, eyes full of panic.

"Behind the church," Norman said. "No, wait. Over there, by the manger."

The desperados hurried to the stable set up for the Live Nativity Scene the next night. There were no animals or figures, only the lean-to stable, an empty manger crib with loose straw in it, and a few bales of hay which they crouched behind.

The police car sailed by without slowing.

"I'm cold and tired," Nathan said, huddling. "And the stupid turkey is heavy and I want to go home." In nearly two hours they had traveled less than two miles from home.

"Are you sure?" Norman asked. "I mean, we'll probably get punished."

"If we hurry," Nathan said, "we can get home before Dad. Maybe we'll just get punished for the cake."

Norman looked pensive a moment, then said, "Okay, let's go."

"But what about this?" Nathan asked, nodding at the turkey in his lap.

"It'll slow us down," Norman said. "You want to get back before Dad, don't you?"

"Yes," Nathan said weakly. "But—"

"Put it in the crib," the older brother said. "It'll stay frozen out here. Leave the blanket, too."

Nathan left the turkey and the boys hightailed it for home.

It wasn't until that evening that Carol thought about her needlepoint table runner, and although she thought she had left it on the car seat, she wasn't a hundred percent sure. She might have set it down somewhere in the house. She was upset, but not frantic, and trusted it would turn up.

***

The next day was Christmas Eve, and in the late afternoon Elsa, one of the two women who cleaned the Catholic Church, came to Father Murphy as he was preparing for a five o'clock mass.

"Father, I found this in the confessional this morning," she said. "I think it slipped down behind the seat and somebody forgot it." She handed him a Raggedy Ann doll.

"Oh, nuts," Father Jack said, remembering how distraught Millie Hampton had been. "I know whose it is. She'll be missing it. I'll call her after this mass. I can give it to her at nine when she comes for the Live Nativity." He tucked the Raggedy Ann doll under his vestments and into his pants belt so he'd be sure not to forget it.

* * *

The Methodist Church bathrobes-and-broom-sticks pageant went about as expected. Not perfect, of course—a rowdy angel pushed her off-balance Wise-Man/brother into the manger—but it fell within the parameters of a successful presentation. Parents and grandparents loved it. And it finished in plenty of time for Tom and Carol to eat a late supper and drive up the road to the Catholic Church for Father Jack's Live Nativity Scene.

The actors had gathered in the church and an overflow crowd huddled together in the parking lot in the bitter cold.

"Father," someone called. "Father Murphy. Bad news. The Logans called. The Baby Jesus has a slight fever and they don't dare take him out in this cold. The fever came up very suddenly. They were very apologetic."

Father Jack pulled off his glasses and rubbed the bridge of his nose with his thumb and forefinger. When he opened his eyes again, he smiled.

"Okay," he said to the actors. "Tonight we improvise." Out of his robe, as if by magic, he pulled Raggedy Ann. "Mary, Joseph, meet your new son."

He handed the expectant parents the doll and they wrapped it in a towel.

"Let's go, people," Father Jack said. "The show must go on. The faithful await."

Father Jack's Live Nativity was magnificent. It proceeded smoothly, beautifully, everyone coming in on cue, including the ox (which had been a concern to some).

Pastor Tom was so filled with awe at the beauty of it that he didn't feel the rivalry.

Then, at the curtain call when the pageant finished, Father Jack strode up to the manger to make an announcement. He asked Mary and Joseph for the doll, then looked out onto the crowd and saw Millie Hampton and her daughter Megan.

"Folks, I give you the actor who tonight filled in at the last minute as the Baby Jesus—Raggedy Ann." He held up the doll.

"The Logan baby, whom we pray for now, ran a little fever and couldn't be here. So, who more appropriate than Raggedy Ann, whom we all know and love, and who literally has written on her heart what our Lord Jesus has on his: *I love you.*"

Father Jack showed the doll's heart to the people, the words *I love you* stitched on its heart. "For this special evening we give thanks and bless this doll, which is a Christmas present from a very special mother, Millie Hampton, to her very special daughter, Megan. Millie and Megan, thank you from our church and the whole community for letting us borrow Raggedy Ann tonight."

The Hamptons came up and Father Jack presented Megan with her Christmas doll.

"Merry Christmas," he said, and hugged both mother and daughter.

"Hey," interrupted the girl playing Mary. "Look, Father. There's a turkey in here. *There's a turkey in the manger.*"

Mary and Joseph lifted the frozen twelve pound turkey out of the Baby Jesus's crib. Without stumbling over a word, Father Jack said, "Ah, the surprise!" He reached and took the turkey—was this *his* answered prayer or *Millie's?*—turned and handed it to Millie Hampton.

"With deepest appreciation, Millie!" he said. "Christmas dinner."

He never missed a beat, Pastor Tom marveled. *My friend Jack, steady under pressure.*

Then the boy playing Joseph said, "Father, what about this blanket? It was in the crib, too."

Father Jack held up the needlepointed blanket before the people like a matador holding a cape before a bull. "It's lovely," he said, remembering that Millie Hampton was a seamstress with little to give except her labor.

Carol Smith meanwhile looked to Tom as their friend continued, on a roll.

"This fine gift is from someone who wishes to remain anonymous," he said. "Consider the intricate needlework, the time and love that went into it. And the pattern—*a cross and a flame*—the cross to remind us of the Baby Jesus's eventual fate that benefits us, and a flame to signify perhaps the Holy Spirit but also a campfire to warm the Christmas babe on a night such as he was born. This thoughtful gift shall become a part of our creche from this night on, a comforter to swaddle those babies who'll comes forth to play the Baby Jesus in years ahead."

Carol looked at Tom, their eyes laughing, their faces grinning broadly.

Nathan and Norman Fellows stared at each other incredulously.

Millie Hampton began to clap, and Father Jack hugged her again, sure she was pleased with so much in one night—her handmade doll blessed after playing Jesus, a Christmas turkey in her arms, her needlework finding a home in the manger crib.

"Will you tell him?" Carol said to Tom. "About the Methodist logo?"

Tom chuckled, shook his head. "Nope," he said. "Unless you want it back."

"No," she said. "It's a good place for it."

Tom looked as if he was ready to explode with laughter.

"Then you won't be able to rub it in," Carol said. "You realize that, don't you?"

"Yup," he said. "But that's okay. This is *better* than bowling. *I'll know.*"

As Carol and Tom turned their attention back to the manger, Father Jack declared from scripture, "Unto us a child is born, a Son is given." And as the priest uttered the words, Carol Smith thought she felt a leaping in her womb. Which indeed she did. She and Tom would have a healthy baby boy eight months later. And a year from that very night, little Jack Smith, swaddled in a Methodist needlepoint table runner, would become the first Protestant baby to play the Baby Jesus in the Catholic Church's Live Nativity Scene.

***

The Logan baby was fully recovered by Christmas morning and was eating breakfast about the same time Millie Hampton rose to prepare her twelve-pound Christmas turkey for roasting. When Millie reached into the turkey's center cavity to remove the plastic package of innards, out came another plastic bag. In it was a certificate: *Lucky Christmas Winner may claim one thousand dollars at the IGA.* She paid her house taxes.

***

Pastor Tom still bowls for the Holy Rollers. And he continues to strive to tie or beat his good friend Jack Murphy's score. Their rivalry, like sibling rivalry, is still there, always will be. But as more love moves into the foreground, the rivalry becomes less important.

***

Prayers are funny things, aren't they? Especially Christmas prayers. Wants, wishes, heartfelt yearnings, thoughts, whispers, all apparently qualify. And many are answered. Yes indeed, prayers are funny things.

Christmas Eve, 12 Plus 97

Every year until I was twelve Nana Antonia and I shared a birthday, October 28th. On our last birthday together the years totaled a hundred and nine—my twelve plus her ninety-seven.

That was also the year it snowed here in Vermont every day in December, right up until Christmas Eve, when it finally stopped and the night was flooded by the light of a full moon. Athough the calendar on the wall said that night was December 24, 1961, I'll always date it by Nana Antonia's and my birthday year—Christmas Eve, 12 Plus 97.

Nana Antonia wasn't my grandmother, she was my great-grandmother, my father's grandmother. I was born on her eighty-fifth birthday, and they say even then she was fit, keen-minded, vital.

Shortly after I was born, my grandparents, whom I don't remember—my father's parents, Nana Antonia's son and daughter-in-law—were killed in a collision with a moose in New Hampshire while on their way home. The loss was hard on everyone, but because ours was a family farm, the two deaths dealt a double whammy, the farm losing half its labor force in the blink of an eye. Mom said Dad walked woodenly through his chores, and had it not been for neighbors pitching in, she wonders if the farm might-n't have failed.

So Nana Antonia moved in, partly to care for me while my parents worked the farm, but also to avoid facing the ghosts in the empty house she and my grandparents had shared. Her moving in was a closing of ranks that helped the three of them share the unimaginable weight of emptiness. Their grief is something I don't remember seeing out in the open those early years. Thank God for the blinders of childhood.

What I do remember is Nana Antonia always being there for me, holding me on her lap, rocking me, reading to me, listening to me. I especially remember her laugh—that joyous, head-back, porcelain-teeth-rattling laugh. She called her dentures her china teeth.

"Same material as my old dinner plates, Billy," she'd say, "fine china." They sat in a glass of water on her bedside table every night, a fact I didn't catch onto for awhile.

"Watch this," she'd say when I was small, and with a click and a flick—no hands—she'd stick out her tongue and deliver her uppers to me. Before I could reach for her tongue and touch them, she'd flick again, they'd clack back into place, and she'd smile a broad, toothy grin. To a child who didn't know false teeth existed, this was magic. My Nana Antonia was magic.

Once, in the kitchen, our two cats Gladys and Marvin were pawing a catnip mouse on the linoleum floor. Our yellow Lab pup, Pumpkin, decided to join the fun. He jumped forward, overturning the silver water bowl so it trapped the catnip mouse like pheasant under glass.

Gladys, Marvin, and Pumpkin knew where the disappeared mouse was, but the water bowl, riding a film of spilled water, clung to the linoleum. Pumpkin barked as the cats swatted at it. Before long all three were going crazy, nosing and batting the silver dome around the wet floor like a hockey puck. Nana Antonia and I howled until our sides ached and tears flowed. My Nana Antonia loved to laugh.

She loved to tell about a Christmas party she attended the year before I was born, when she was eighty-four. She'd gone with some church ladies to sing Christmas carols at the Old Folks Home. After they sang, Nana Antonia stepped up to the refreshment table and dipped her cup into a huge bowl to get some Christmas punch, a standard mix of fruit juice and ginger ale, with sherbet and ice cubes on top and lemon wedges for flavor. But when she leaned over, ladle in one hand, punch cup in the other, her glasses slid down her nose. Hoping to jolt them back, she snapped her head up. The glasses hopped back, but her china teeth—"bottom choppers"—flew out of her mouth and plopped into the punch.

"So what'd you do?" I asked.

"Reached in and felt around, like fishing for a spoon in dishwater," she said.

"And you found 'em?" I asked.

"Not right away," she said. "I was in such a hurry that I thought I had 'em first try. It was icy and my hand was getting numb. I thought someone was coming, so I panicked and popped 'em in my mouth. Only it wasn't them. It was—"

I could see she was close to breaking into her window-glass-rattling laugh then.

"—a lemon wedge!" she said, sucking in her cheeks, rolling her lips over her teeth. "Did I ever pucker!"

We howled, and every time our laughing subsided, Nana Antonia would pucker and we'd be off to the races again. She loved to laugh and she loved to tell stories.

My father had also enjoyed a close relationship with his grandmother, Nana Antonia. And because she filled in for my own deceased grandmother, his mother, in a sense my father and I shared the same grandmother.

When Dad was seven, an ornery bull trapped him in the bullpen, where he oughtn't have been. He'd fallen from the fence. Nana Antonia was at the clothesline whomping the dust out of an old rag rug with her violin-shaped wire rug-beater when she heard him scream. Still clutching the rug-beater, she ran to the bull pen, vaulted the six-foot fence in a handspring, and confronted the bull. And, as my mother told the story, "Nana Antonia commenced to beat every particle of dust out of that poor old bull while your father made his escape."

"I should've used the rug beater to tan your father's hide instead of that poor bull's," Nana always added.

Every year for our shared birthday, Mom would bake a cake and squiggle our names on it, Antonia and Billy, then cover it with an army of candles, the sum of our ages—five plus ninety, six plus ninety-one, seven plus ninety-two—each year adding two candles. That went on until 1961, 12 plus 97. That year I blew out the candles for both of us. Nana Antonia was too short of breath.

By Thanksgiving she lay confined to bed, barely able to walk without help. Barely two months earlier she had seemed hale and hearty, walking to and from the mail box at the end of our driveway or surveying the pumpkin patch behind the barn. Now she was losing strength fast, as Doc Whitney's house calls confirmed.

"Winding down," Doc Whitney said. "Antonia's ninety-seven, and she's simply winding down."

Like a grandfather clock? I thought. *So why can't we wind her up again?* But I knew it was hopeless. My Nana Antonia was dying.

"I think it's a cancer," she said one morning as I cleared away her dishes. She had eaten almost nothing. "My hips ache and I can feel something growing inside me, taking over my stomach, squeezing my lungs."

"Cancer?" I said dully, setting the tray aside so I could sit on the edge of her bed. My face muscles wouldn't work, and my eyes felt hot and watery.

"Yes, Billy," she said. "It means I'm going to die."

I glanced away.

"We all die sometime," she said.

I couldn't look at her. Finally, after a long silence, she reached to cup her warm hand to my cheek.

"Billy," she said. "I'm ninety-seven. That's almost a hundred years old, a century. That's pretty amazing, don't you think?"

I nodded but couldn't keep my lips from pressing tightly together.

"I've had a good, beautiful life. I've laughed, cried, loved." She pointed to a framed needlework sampler above her bureau. "Get that, will you?" she said.

I retrieved it, handed it to her. Stitched on the burlap were the words *Live until you die*. She handed it back.

"I want you to have it," she said. "A friend made it when I turned fifty. I was feeling old that day and it cheered me up. I hung it over my bureau as a reminder."

On the first of December I carried Nana Antonia's breakfast up to her bedroom.

"Is it snowing?" she asked.

"I don't think so," I said, pulling up the shade. "Well, yes, it is," I said. "Flurries."

"Isn't it lovely?" she said.

"Yes," I said. "Peaceful." I tied the fabric curtains back and helped her sit up against a couple of pillows.

"Good chance we'll have a white Christmas," I said.

"Oh, I hope so," Nana Antonia answered, eyes showing more spark than I'd seen in days. "I love white Christmases."

It snowed a little every day after that, and I wondered if we weren't setting a record for consecutive snow days. So long as it snowed outside, Nana

Antonia managed to hold her own inside.

By the third week in December I had begun to associate snow with her staying alive, thinking perhaps it sustained her. Every night at bedtime I prayed for snow, and every morning I awoke and walked to the window first thing to see if it had. And every day Nana Antonia awoke and took a little breakfast.

"When your grandfather was young," she said one morning, speaking of her son who had died in the car crash, "and the streets and fields were covered with snow like this, we'd hitch up the horse, a huge Percheron named Clyde, and we'd all ride in the cutter, our sleigh."

Nana Antonia had told me that story many times when I was younger, as she had doubtless told it to my father when he was a boy. When telling it to me, she had always lifted me onto her lap in the rocking chair by the woodstove, where we'd pretend to hold the reins, singing *Jingle Bells* over and over as our sleigh glided over hills and fields of fresh-fallen snow. I had never been in a horse-drawn sleigh, but because of Nana Antonia's lap, I felt as if I had.

Reverend Dodd stopped by weekly to see Nana Antonia, who insisted he update her on the happenings of church and town. He told her of the plans for the Christmas Eve candlelight service which always packed the small white clapboard church. Where forty attended on Sundays, Christmas Eve drew two hundred.

"Of course, the Fire Marshal has sent his usual letter warning about open flames in the church," Reverend Dodd said. "I brought the concern to the

Board of Deacons. But as happens every year, someone said, 'Haven't burned the place down in two
hundred years.' So the Deacons voted to do it the
way we've always done it."

"Must've been Harley Silk said that, right?" Nana
Antonia said. "Harley always says that about not having burned it down in two hundred years."

She chuckled at that, and when Reverend Dodd
joined in, I thought Nana Antonia seemed stronger,
more animated, energized by the laughter. A pause
followed their laughter, after which Nana Antonia
said, "I wish I could be there Christmas Eve."

The minister bit his lip, dropped his gaze to his
lap. He looked up and said, "Why not ask Doc
Whitney?"

This Dodd oughta change his name, I thought, *to
Dodge.* It seemed to me he had sidestepped Nana
Antonia's question, and her yearning.

"Good suggestion," she said, sensing his discom-
fort. "I'll do that. Maybe I'll see you then, for
Christmas Eve."

I showed him out, and by the time I got back up
to Nana Antonia's room, she had drifted off to sleep
even though she had napped for two hours before the
minister's visit.

I looked out the window and realized it was late
afternoon and it hadn't yet snowed. I prayed for an
evening snowfall, even a few isolated flakes as I looked
at my sleeping great-grandmother. She was losing
strength and stamina faster than I'd realized.

"But we can wrap her in blankets and carry her
in," I argued at the supper table that night.

"No," my father said emphatically, almost angrily. "It's not a good idea."

"But what if Doc Whitney says it's okay?"

"No," Dad repeated.

"Why not?" I said.

My father looked flustered, frustrated. He and I seldom argued, but I refused to give ground this time.

"Well?" I pressed.

My father's face reddened. He drew a deep, audible breath, his barrel chest swelling.

"Dad!" I whined. "Why not?"

"Because the cold air could kill her!" he blurted, standing up quickly so his chair scraped the floor and tipped over. He wadded his napkin, threw it on his plate, and stormed out of the kitchen.

My mother, who hadn't said a word, said, "He's upset. Don't forget, Billy, your father loves Nana Antonia, too. She's always been in his life. This is hard for him."

I heard what my mother was saying, but I wasn't sure why she was saying it. If Dad loved Nana Antonia, why wouldn't he help her go to the candlelight service? As Nana herself had said, she was dying. Like it or not—and I didn't—Nana Antonia was dying.

"He's not mad at you, Billy," Mom said. "He's angry that he's going to lose his grandmother."

I didn't know what to do. There was no arguing with my father, so I retrieved Nana Antonia's needlework sampler from my bed stand, carried it to my parents' bedroom, and laid it on my father's pillow.

There was nothing else I could do. Except pray for snow.

Doc Whitney visited the next day, saying the decision about Christmas Eve was up to the family—meaning Dad. Doc said it depended how weak she was and the state of her lungs. What Dad had said was true—the chilly air could be too much for her. And, Doc said, church could mean a chance of her picking up a cold or the flu from holiday visitors.

Dad said we would wait and see. Whenever he said that, it meant no.

Christmas Eve morning arrived. Nana Antonia was very weak, barely able to speak above a whisper. She could hardly draw breath and her hands shook when she raised a spoonful of oatmeal. I was sure Dad knew how poorly she was doing.

I did my chores early that afternoon. It gave me something to do. Only once did I ask my father if he had decided, and he said, "I'm thinking, I'm thinking."

It hadn't snowed all day.

Supper was quiet. After we finished our pumpkin pie and cleared the dishes, Mom said, "So. Shall we get ready for church?"

I looked at Dad, his face tight, worried. I didn't move. I just looked across the kitchen table at him, seeing him in a way I'd never seen him before, knowing in that exact moment how afraid he was of losing his grandmother, our Nana Antonia. Tears filled my eyes, and as he looked back at me, tears filled his, too.

Finally he swallowed and said, "I'll warm up the car. You and Mom help Nana Antonia get dressed."

I sprang from my chair and bounded up the stairs two at a time.

"The snow's started," Nana Antonia said when I entered her room. "Perfect for the candlelight service." She was sitting on the edge of her bed by herself.

"Dad said we're taking you, too!" I blurted.

"I knew he would," she said, winking. "Your mother ironed my outfit this afternoon."

An hour later we were driving to the church on the hill, Nana Antonia bundled in two quilts on the back seat between Mom and me. Dad pulled up by the front door and went in to find the church's wheelchair. He got the three of us inside and went back out to park the car.

The service began. The place was packed.

Nana Antonia, Mom, and I sat in a front pew, saving room for Dad. The first hymn ended and I saw Mom glancing around anxiously. Where was my father? It couldn't take that long to park the car.

Reverend Dodd read several old Testament scriptures. Then we had prayer concerns, and a few names of the sick were mentioned, plus three boys in the military. Reverend Dodd waited to see if anyone had anything to add under either Joys or Concerns.

After a moment a voice a few pews back said, "I am thankful to have Antonia Hartness here with us tonight. Mrs. Hartness, I understand, recently celebrated her ninety-seventh birthday."

Everyone applauded. And my great-grandmother, one quilt around her shoulders, another across her lap, raised a shaky hand in acknowledgment. Then, in a voice stronger than I imagined she could muster, she said, "That sounds like Harley Silk. Harley, let's be careful with these candles. Don't want to burn down this church now, do we?"

To which Harley Silk answered, as if the two of them were engaged in a familiar holiday litany, "Haven't burned it down in more'n two hundred years."

The congregation erupted in laughter.

Someone read Luke's Christmas Gospel and we sang carols, including *Angels We Have Heard on High* and *It Came Upon a Midnight Clear*. But as Reverend Dodd launched into his sermon, my father's seat was still empty. It was clear from my mother's glances that she had no more idea of his whereabouts than I did. Finally I leaned Nana Antonia over onto Mom and whispered, "Be right back. I'll see if Dad's changing a flat."

Our car was nowhere to be seen. I reasoned my father had either gone to Randolph for something or back to the house. Maybe he feared the candlelight service would be too emotional. I walked back inside and sat by Nana Antonia as the lights went out for the candlelighting.

Nana Antonia lit hers off Mom's. I could see her wrinkled face light up. She looked tired, but her smile glowed. I lit my candle from hers and passed the flame on. When everyone's candle had been lighted, Reverend Dodd led us in *Silent Night*, which we sang *a cappella*. The small church felt warm and safe.

Reverend Dodd pronounced the benediction and people stood to wish one another Merry Christmas.

Many folks crowded around Nana Antonia to say hello.

Gradually everyone funnelled past Reverend Dodd and out to the snow-covered dooryard.

"The snow's stopped," someone said.

"And the moon's full!" said another.

Balanced on the horizon before us sat a huge golden coin. That's when we heard the jingle bells signaling the approach of a horse-drawn sleigh, a red-and-green cutter with two bench seats, pulled by a huge-footed horse.

And perched atop the driver's seat, reins in his hands, sat my father, grinning broadly. The crowd babbled its delight as Dad drove the sleigh up to the church door and looked down at Nana Antonia in the wheelchair.

"Someone call for an old-fashioned sleigh ride?" Dad asked, stepping down. His eyes twinkled as he slid his strong arms under Nana Antonia and lifted her into the passenger seat. Mom and I scrambled on board and bookended her, draping the quilts around her. In no time we were whooshing down the road.

I don't recall Nana Antonia's face when she died two weeks later, barely into 1962. What I remember is that night, Mom and me giddy with cold, Dad snapping the reins, the sleigh skimming the moonlit snow. What I remember is my great-grandmother, Nana Antonia, eyes dancing and head back as her joyful, china-teeth-rattling laugh cracked the chilly air and echoed over the Vermont hillsides. What I remember is a face—an old woman's face, filled with pure, *live-until-you-die* delight—on that last

Christmas Eve she was among us, in the year we all shared, in the year 12 Plus 97.

One Maine Christmas

"Whoa now! Hold it! Perley, DJ, James. Stop horsing around back there. We're down to two practices before the Nativity pageant, and I want us to get it right."

Mr. Gamage, the Sunday school superintendent, had a way of getting order without yelling. It was a gift he had. Now he stood at an easel and wrote on a pad with a Magic Marker that was going dry.

"Perley Alley," Mr. Gamage said. "Would you please go to the Sunday School cabinet and get me a fresh Magic Marker? There's a new package on the top shelf."

Perley was back in a flash, handing the Magic Marker to Mr. Gamage, who thanked him and continued on.

"Okay, one more walk-through and we can call it a day. Places, everyone. Mary, Joseph, angels, shepherds, wise guys—lights, camera, action!"

James, Perley, and DJ walked home together from the church. James hardly spoke.

"Whatsa matter, James?" DJ asked. "You're like my sister when she didn't get asked to the prom."

James was glad to have these two friends. DJ and Perley meant a lot to him, because acceptance had been slow in coming since he'd arrived on the cove. He didn't know if it because he was new in school or because he was the only black kid—the only black *person*—in this Maine coastal village. His dad was the new preacher and they had been in the parsonage barely five months.

James had been adopted at four months, and now that he was ten, he'd been experiencing a gnawing, something more than simple curiosity, to learn about his history and to claim his black heritage. With that gnawing came a sense of alienation, of differentness.

Although no one mistreated him, James was painfully aware he was the solitary black in a coastal village made up of generation upon generation of white lobstermen, white loggers, and white blueberry rakers.

"Yeah, James," Perley added, curly red hair unmoving in the breeze. "What's buggin' you?"

James looked at his freckled, pale-faced friend, hesitant to answer.

"Well?" DJ pressed, his long blond hair rippling like cornsilk across his eyebrows. He swept at it futilely. "Something's up, James. This ain't you."

"I dunno," James answered, realizing his friends had caught him sleepwalking. "Guess I must be homesick for our last home."

This was only a half-lie. He did miss the friends he'd had back when his Dad had been a seminary student. Between seminary families and the kids he'd known in elementary school, he'd had quite a few friends, several of whom were black children.

"Maybe it's because it's close to Christmas,"

James added, smiling weakly. His two new friends let him drop the subject and the three of them split up for home.

The next day at practice everybody walked through their parts as Mr. Gamage narrated the script for the pantomime Nativity. Each actor listened closely for cues.

"And while they were there, the time came for Mary to be delivered. And she gave birth to her first-born son and wrapped him in swaddling cloths, and laid him in a manger, because there was no place for them in the inn."

DJ, playing Joseph, watched as Mary, whose name really was Mary, placed the swaddled doll in a crib of weathered lobster-trap slats which Mr. Gamage had filled with straw.

Tears streamed down James's cheeks, shining like silver ski tracks on his dark skin. DJ motioned Perley to look, and the two of them stared at James. Nothing was said until the three of them were walking home.

"What was that all about, James?" asked DJ.

"What was *what* about?" James said.

"We saw you," Perley said.

"Saw me *what*?" James said sharply.

Perley and DJ backed away, staring at a red-faced James.

"I don't think anybody else saw," Perley said.

James relaxed his hunched shoulders. "I'm not exactly sure what happened," he said.

The three of them continued walking.

"Musta been something," said DJ.

"C'mon. You can tell us," Perley said. "We're you're best friends, ain't we, James?"

They stopped walking, and James stared blankly out on the blue-green waters of the cove, then up at the slate gray sky. He pondered the question and the trust level.

Perley's soft brown eyes were as inviting as a pile of raked autumn leaves.

James let his breath out loudly, not realizing he'd been holding it. With the outrush of breath came the loosening of his tongue.

"It was that story," he said.

"What story?" asked DJ.

"You know. Mr. Gamage's story."

"I think he means the Baby Jesus story," interrupted Perley. "Right, James?"

"Yeah," James answered. "I could *feel* it, the alone feeling of being in a strange town. It made me feel sad. Being all alone like that, in that manger, it musta been terrible lonely for the baby."

"But he had parents, James," DJ said.

Perley simply listened.

"I bet they were lonely, too," countered James. "They didn't know anybody."

Silence. DJ was finally at a loss for words.

"You feel lonely, James?" asked Perley. A foghorn moaned beyond the cove.

"Lots," James said. Silence again, and the foghorn.

"But ain't we your friends?" DJ asked.

"Yeah," James said. "But—"

"But *what?*" snapped DJ.

Perley waited.

"But—" James said, "I'm ... I'm ... black."

Again the foghorn.

"We know that, James," said DJ. "It's not exact-ly something you can hide around here, is it? It's a small town. Newcomers stand out. Besides, what's being black got to do with it?"

Perley listened as James tried to explain to DJ.

"I'm the only black person in this entire place, DJ," he said, "including my parents, who are white. Don't you see? You've always been here, always been a part of things. You don't know what it is to be dif-ferent or lonely. It's just not the same for me. It's very different."

DJ shook his head yes, even though he didn't really understand, and Perley said nothing.

79

Pageant night arrived, and the church overflowed with parents and grandparents eager to watch the young actors recreate the story of the first Christmas. James' father flitted among the people, shaking hands, smiling, inviting people to Sunday morning services. The children giggled nervously as they took their places.

James' father offered an opening prayer, Mr. Gamage made the introductions and praised the kids for their hard work, then thanked the mothers for helping with costumes.

The drama began. Shepherds' staffs clunked the floor loudly as they marched in. Angels burst out from behind the old upright piano, tin-foil wings snagging other angels' halos. Mr. Gamage stumbled over the name Quirinius—which he'd always gotten right in practice—this time adding a syllable and pronouncing it "Qui-nin-rin-ius." Otherwise things proceeded without a hitch.

DJ and Mary trekked down the center aisle leading their cardboard donkey, arriving at the Bethlehem manger. The betrothed couple, Mary bulging with pillow, knelt behind the straw-filled lobster-trap crib.

The organist played *We Three Kings of Orient Are* as the Three Wise Men arrived via the side aisle bearing their gold, frankincense, and myrrh. James walked second in the caravan, typecast as a shining black Abyssinian Prince carrying his gift. The Three Wise Men approached the manger crib and fell to their knees before the newborn King.

When the last gift was laid down, the entire cast leaned forward as Mary drew back the swaddling cloths that covered the babe. But the other children's eyes weren't on the Christ child. They were on James, who knelt staring open-mouthed into the crib. After a moment he turned his face up toward them and managed a tight-lipped grin. Tears welled up in his eyes.

He looked into the manger crib again to be certain. Yes, he'd seen correctly. The Bethlehem Babe lay there, all right. But this doll was different from the one he'd seen at practice, for this one's plastic body shone black—streaked and smeared and carefully colored in black Magic Marker.

DJ leaned forward and whispered, "James, looks like you're not the only black kid in *this* town any more." As he said it, he and Perley each placed a hand beside James' on the edge of the crib.

The lump in James' throat wouldn't let him swallow, try as he might. That's when he saw the black stains on DJ's and Perley's fingertips, Magic Marker stains from their small hands gripping the markers in pencil-fashion too near the tip.

"You're right," James whispered back hoarsely, nodding toward his two friends' fingers on the crib. "Counting Jesus, there's four of us."

"At least four," Perley said. Which was when the other children leaned in and laid their writing hands on the crib. Each hand's fingertips were stained black, stained black from gripping—pencil-fashion, too near the tip—what had been left in Mr. Gamage's box of Sunday school markers.

James couldn't help but break into a broad grin.

Cameras flashed and the cast stood to take its bows. People who remember say that year's pageant was the best ever for pictures.

Christmas Special Delivery

"Who's taking care of Clyde's cat while he's in the hospital?" asked the tall man standing in front of the Orient General Store.

An older man sat on the front step, feet flat on the sidewalk, elbows on his knees. A trail of aromatic smoke—the sweet smell of cherry—drifted up out of the handsome brown pipe in his mouth, and his lips made a dry puck-puck sound as they drew smoke in through the curved mouthpiece.

"Clyde's cat?" He gave a puzzled look and kept puck-pucking on his pipe, hardly looking up at the question-asker. Then, as if an afterthought, he said, "Oh, you're referring to Sardine?"

"Of course he means Sardine, Delbert P. Coffin," came his wife's sharp voice from behind him. "You were going to play your little guessing game with Tink, weren't you, dear?" she said impatiently.

Delbert Coffin's cheeks never moved, though his lips continued to pull on the pipe. He said nothing.

"Well?" the big woman demanded, hands on her hips. "You gonna to tell Tink about the cat or not?"

Delbert paused a second too long, so his wife Velma turned to the tall man and explained, "Sardine's at the vet's, Tink, until Clyde gets out of the hospital. It's a tossup which one of them will be released first, but if Sardine gets the okay to go home, Delbert and I can board him at our place until Clyde's out and about."

Sardine was Clyde the postmaster's cat. Clyde's fall from a stepladder while painting the bottom of his boat had left him with two broken legs and Sardine with a fractured pelvis.

Everyone in Orient knew Clyde Daggett. He'd been the small town's postmaster for thirty-five years. And they all knew Sardine, a stray cat who showed up at the Post Office out of nowhere one day. Whenever you stopped in for your mail, there would be Clyde smiling and ready to help at the mail window, and there on the counter, in a cardboard box that once held five hundred sheets of letterhead, lay Sardine curled up and comfortable, often asleep. The Post Office Cat, everyone called him. He even made the front cover of the *Suffolk Times*, eastern Long Island's weekly newspaper, peering lazily over the lip of the box. The Post Office Cat quickly caught on, a curiosity to visitors and a fixture in the community, almost as much a fixture as Clyde himself.

Clyde Daggett knew everybody and had helped more people with zip codes and Christmas packages "than Carter's has pills", as he used to say. Never missed a day of work for sickness, amazing in itself considering how many germs he came in contact with each day. But now he was laid up at Eastern Long Island Hospital five miles away in Greenport.

"Then who's taking over the Nativity pageant?" Tink asked, this time directing his question at Velma.

"Karen Sweeney, the minister's wife," she said. "She's quite capable."

"The show must go on, Tink," interjected Delbert matter-of-factly without looking up, never missing a puck-puck on his pipe.

"Oh, Delbert," Velma half-whined. "It's not a show, it's a *pageant*. A Nativity pageant is very different from a show."

Delbert looked up, winked at Tink, and said to his wife, "That's what you think, Velly. When them kids get into that pulpit and the little ones get to squirming, it's a show!"

Tink laughed out loud and Velma Coffin stifled a laugh and pretended to look stern. She finally succumbed, however, and began to giggle.

"I suppose so, Delbert," she said. "They are cute, aren't they?"

"Cute don't half describe it," he said. "Remember the time our Jimmy was a shepherd and lost his hold on that wooden crook?"

"And it bounced off Mother Mary's head?" Velma added.

"And knocked the frankincense out of the King's hand?" Delbert said.

"Which fell into the manger and spilled that god-awful perfume all over," she said, the two of them beginning to cackle at this newly remembered litany.

"And remember poor old Reverend Longley the next Sunday? He could barely get through the sermon because his eyes were watering so," Delbert said.

"And the stink," Tink chimed in. "I can still smell it when we shampoo the carpet by the pulpit."

Delbert Coffin held the pipe in his hand, alternately laughing and coughing now.

The commotion attracted the attention of three old ladies who were leaving the Post Office next door.

"What's going on, Velma?" one of them asked. "Delbert okay?"

"Is it a heart attack?" asked one of the others.

"Shall we call the Rescue Squad?" asked the third.

But when the ladies saw that Velma's eyes were filled not with fear but with laughter, they relaxed.

"No, thank you," she told them. "Delbert is fine, at least in a manner of speaking. A little odd perhaps, but healthwise he's fine." Then she added, "We were just reminiscing about past pageants at the church."

"Oh," said one of the ladies, Eunice Davis. "We were talking about that with Inez Marsh in the Post Office. Our Sardine wasn't in his box on the counter, so Inez told us what happened. Then Trisha, that young fill-in Postmistress from Riverhead, said she's had maybe hundreds of people in asking about Clyde and our Post Office cat."

Velma nodded her head. "Good to hear folks are concerned," she said.

"And what about the Nativity pageant? Is it still on?" Euny Davis continued. "I mean, with Clyde in the hospital. After all, he's directed the pageants for—oh gosh, must be thirty years. About as long as he's been postmaster, I'd guess."

When Euny Davis paused to take a breath, Tink shared his newly gained information. "The pastor's wife is directing," he said.

Euny Davis and her two friends went silent. It was as if a brick had dropped from the roof and crashed on the sidewalk in front of the General Store.

"How's *Clyde* going to feel about *that?*" Eunice Davis said, a degree of snappiness in her voice.

Delbert Coffin looked blankly at his wife Velma, then at his friend Tink, then back at his wife. "I don't know," he said, knowing better than to get into it. He passed the buck. "How do *you* think he'll feel about it, Velma?"

Velma Coffin's face took on a fretful look.

"I don't think—" she said, measuring her words, "I don't think Clyde will mind someone else directing in a pinch. But it'll be hard on him to not be there. After all, night after tomorrow's the pageant, and he'll have to spend it in the hospital."

"And without his cat," Tink chimed in. "I feel sorry for him." And everyone nodded their agreement.

* * *

"Merry Christmas, Clyde."

Clyde Daggett looked up from his hospital bed. He had been in a half-sleep, and hearing his name had surprised him.

"Oh, hi, Delbert," he said, shaking his head to clear away his cobwebs. "Uhh, Merry Christmas to you, too." He pulled on the adjustment lever at the side of his bed, raising himself to the sitting position. "But it's still a few days until Christmas, I believe."

"Well, yes, it is," Tink said from the doorway

behind Delbert. "But we figured since it was pageant night and you couldn't make it to the church to direct, you'd be feeling a bit out of sorts."

"*Depressed*, Tink, *depressed* is what you mean to say," Delbert corrected. He shook his head in mock disgust. "*Out of sorts* is advertising talk for—you know, diarrhea or constipation. If Clyde can't make the play, he feels *depressed*, not out of sorts."

"All right, all right," the man in the hospital bed interjected. "I'm not out of sorts and I'm not depressed. I'm what the kids today call *bummed out*. I'm bummed out. I missed the pageant, I miss work, and I miss my Sardine."

After an awkward moment, Delbert said, pointing to Clyde's two leg casts, "You taking autographs?"

"People still do that?" Clyde asked.

"I don't know about other people, but *this* people still do," Delbert said, withdrawing a pen from his shirt pocket and making an exaggerated flourish with his writing hand over one of the casts.

"Careful, careful," Clyde said, only half-kidding. "That one's already broken in two places, and the other in three, so I don't need you falling on me."

Delbert and Tink each signed the two casts.

"So. How's it going here, Clyde?" Delbert asked, sitting on the edge of the bed.

"Food's good," the postmaster said. "Nurses are nice. Bedpans are room temperature unless they've just washed them."

Delbert and Tink laughed.

"Everyone misses you down to the Post Office," Tink said.

"Tell 'em I miss them, too," Clyde said. "Look at all those cards on the window sill, and there's five bouquets of flowers there, all from yesterday and today. Folks have been great."

"You deserve it," Delbert said.

"Thanks," Clyde answered. "How's my Sardine?"

"Sardine's fine, just fine," Tink offered. "Well fed. Gets lots of attention. Healing nicely, they say. He's fine."

"I miss him," Clyde said. "I mean, I miss people, too. Don't get me wrong. But Sardine is—well, you know what I mean—*family*."

"Yeah, we know," Tink said. "For us, it was our dog Buddy. When he died two years ago, well ..." His voice trailed off, the wound still somewhat fresh. "Well," he said in a cracking voice, "Margie and me, we still miss him."

The air in the room felt heavy, so Clyde asked, "So how'd the pageant go tonight?" He looked at his wristwatch. "It must be over an hour ago, right?"

Delbert stood up from where he'd been sitting on the edge of the bed and walked to the window. "It went well," he said. "So well that they're talking about taking the show on the road." He drew back the curtain and unlatched the window, pushing it open. "Thank God for first-floor rooms. Here's the road show now."

There on the frosty lawn stood Mary and Joseph and the manger crib. Mary cradled the babe in her arms, a doll swaddled in towels.

Karen Sweeney, the pastor's wife, appeared right outside the window, an open book in her hands. She began to read, and her voice rang out loud and clear. "In those days a decree went out from Caesar Augustus that all the world should be enrolled . . ."

Shepherds, wise men, and angels appeared. When Karen Sweeney read "and a multitude of the heavenly host appeared," more than a hundred people, half of Orient, walked into view to encircle the manger, singing *Hark, the Herald Angels Sing.*

Clyde watched wide-mouthed, after thirty years finally able to enjoy the drama as an observer rather than a director.

Delbert shrugged too, moved by the display of public affection, and said to Clyde, "My friend, you seem to have an embarrassment of riches. People love you."

At a loss for words and close to tears, Clyde said, "I suppose they'll all want to sign my cast?"

To which Delbert retorted, "Well, this is a *cast* party, Clyde."

The moment didn't stay frozen long, for the spell was broken by a voice—not Karen Sweeney's—close by the window.

"Mr. Daggett? Mr. Daggett? You in there?"

It was Buzzy Buswell, whose voice was beginning to change. He was dressed as a shepherd.

"Yes, Buzzy, I'm in here," the postmaster answered.

"Great," the boy said. "Hope you're on your feet again soon. Now sit tight and hold for Special Delivery. Here's a Merry Christmas from a very special sheep!"

In through the window came a familiar box, a box

which once held 500 sheets of letterhead. Delbert received it and passed it along to Clyde. A scrap of wool covered the box, and at one end of it the fleece began to lift. Out peeked a pair of charcoal gray eyes, a tiny wet nose, and furry ears.

"Sardine!" the postmaster said, reaching for the box.

"Be careful," Delbert cautioned. "He's in about the same condition you are, Clyde. And we've only got him out on bail for another couple of hours. The vet wants him in early."

"The vet can wait up for awhile," Clyde said. "Sardine's used to staying up late for David Letterman."

"Meow!" cried the cat in sheep's clothing.

"And a Meow-ry Christmas to you, too!" exclaimed Clyde. He stroked Sardine's neck lightly and tickled his ears. "And Merry Christmas to all of you," Clyde yelled out the window. "Many thanks!"

Outside in the crisp night air more than a hundred voices softly sang "Silent Night, Holy Night, All is calm, all is bright."

No one except Delbert and Tink signed Clyde's casts that night, because by the time the singers had finished *Silent Night,* Clyde the postmaster had fallen fast asleep in his hospital bed with Sardine the Post Office Cat curled in the box on his chest.

Over the next three months nearly three hundred people signed Clyde's two souvenir casts where they hung beside the service window at the Orient Post Office. However, once the story made the papers, more than ten times as many people—all the locals plus thousands of visitors—stopped by to sign the old letterhead box on the counter in which Sardine, the Post Office Cat, spent his days catnapping.

"Someday," Clyde insists, "that box will wind up in the Smithsonian, somewhere between Archie Bunker's arm chair and Mr. Rogers's sweater."

There's no doubt it'll get there, either, because stamped across its end are the words: *Christmas Special Delivery.*

Pastor Cheese's Christmas Eve Communion

What a place to have to spend Christmas Eve—on some little island off the coast of Maine, leading the candlelight service in a dinky church with a group of people he barely knew.

Brad Chesebro wasn't yet a full-fledged, ordained minister. He was a first-semester student at Bangor Seminary, three years from graduation. Yet because so many of Maine's small rural churches couldn't afford resident ministers, despite his inexperience he'd already filled the pulpit four times his first semester. Three of those preaching dates had been at the tiny island church on Fairhaven, a fifteen mile ferry ride from Rockland.

Now, because he had no firm plans to be anywhere for the holidays, he had been asked by the seminary's Field Education Director to go to Fairhaven again, this time to lead their Christmas Eve candlelight service.

When, at age thirty-four, Brad had told the elders at his home church in New York that he wanted to go off to theological school and be a minister, he'd envisioned pastoral ministry as something different from Fairhaven's little podunk chapel. He'd imagined bigger and better things, more like the fifteen-hundred member church of his minister-uncle, the well known, highly respected Dr. Timothy Todd Chesebro. He'd pictured a church with two or three services on Sunday, a semi-professional choir, parishioners galore to shake his hand after church.

Brad's three Sundays at Fairhaven had drawn crowds of twenty-five, twenty-three, twenty-four, respectively. The choir was exactly as his seminary classmates, who had visited there earlier, had described it—three voices: a flat, a sharp, and an undecided. He had to admit one thing, though; the Fairhaven folk were simple, genuine, earthy. After three Sundays he knew this was a group of small-town characters, each unique and different.

Ruthie Phillips was a character, no question about it. In her early fifties, she acted more like an eight year old. She'd been described to Brad as "borderline retarded," lived with her mother. Since she couldn't care for herself, family and friends on Fairhaven kept an eye on her.

Ruthie loved being part of things, especially church, where everybody knew her by name and knew what she was like. Each Sunday Ruthie stood between her mother and her aunt, singing along, hymn book open to the right page. But couldn't read the words. The hymnal was open simply so she'd be like everybody else.

When Brad telephoned Nellie Cook, the organist, with the hymns he'd chosen for his first week, she'd eliminated one and substituted another for it.

"It's not that I can't play it or don't like it,

Reverend Chesebro," she said, despite his protestations that he was not yet entitled to use the title. "And it's not that it wouldn't go with your sermon topic. It's just that—well, *Ruthie doesn't know it.*" That was when Brad had learned Ruthie was "borderline retarded" and that the consensus of the congregation seemed to be to make sure the worship service included hymns Ruthie could sing, too.

Ruthie also loved church because she felt it gave her a job. She arranged the cookies for the refreshments time after every service. There was always a plate or two of wafers that were chocolate on one side and vanilla on the other, perfect for making all sorts of interesting designs.

When that first Sunday came, Brad saw what Nellie Cook meant when she cautioned, "Stand back. Ruthie really belts it out." She belted it out louder than the rest of the small congregation in her shrill, off-key crow's voice that pulled Brad off, too. That annoyed him. So did her calling him—in her thick Down East accent—*Pahstah Cheese,* which everyone else seemed to think was cute and funny. They chuckled whenever she said it.

Brad had been to candlelight services before but had never led one, never planned one. This would be his first.

"We'll supply the candles," Nellie Cook's husband Bob said, speaking for the Board of Deacons. "Nellie can play any of the Christmas carols. You work out the rest."

What the Board of Deacons didn't expect, however, was that Brad would want to make a slight change from the usual.

"Communion?" Bob Cook said. "On Christmas Eve? Pastor Chesebro, the Lord's Supper has never been part of the Christmas Eve candlelight service at Fairhaven."

"Bob, listen. The way I've got it planned, it'll take hardly any more time at all. I can work it in with the candlelighting. The Deacons won't even have to fill or serve or wash the little cups. It'll be a very moving spiritual experience. Trust me." Despite Bob Cook's protests, Brad was insistent.

Christmas Eve arrived. The church was almost full. Evergreen wreaths hung from the lecterns, green garlands strung with bright red cranberries graced the side walls, and a beautifully decorated tree stood in the chancel behind the pulpit. But lovely as it looked to islanders, it looked dull to Brad, a reminder that he was alone and far from home on Christmas Eve. Everyone else had friends, family, *someone*. He had no one.

"You can really pack 'em in, son," Bob said with a wink. "I counted nearly ninety in the sanctuary."

"How many did you have last year?" Brad asked, smiling bravely. He'd have gladly traded numbers for intimacy.

"Oh, about ninety," Bob said with a wink. "Year before, too. The island population tends to be pretty stable in winter."

When the time came for candlelight Communion at the end of the service, Brad instructed people to circle around the outside of all the pews. He had choreographed this and run over it again and again in his mind. First he'd pass the loaf of Nellie's home-baked bread around for each person to rip off a little piece. Then he'd start the silver chalice he'd borrowed from the seminary chapel, inviting everyone to wait for the chalice, then dip their piece of bread into the grape juice and eat it, afterward passing the chalice along to the next person in the huge circle. This, Brad assured the holiday worshipers, would symbolize Christian unity and sharing and lots of other good things.

Everything went smoothly. People circled like a wagon train, just as Brad had planned. He started the bread to the left and each person took a polite piece. Then the chalice started on its way around, passed carefully because the grape juice was more than three-quarters of the way to the rim. People dipped their bread and ate the purple-stained pieces. They were quiet and solemn, almost somber, as if meeting clandestinely in the catacombs like the early Christians. Hardly anybody looked at anybody else.

The chalice was halfway around the circle when the sanctuary's double doors swung open and in stepped Ruthie Phillips, back from arranging the cookies in the Fellowship Hall. Her entrance positioned her directly opposite Brad in the circle. Used to receiving Communion in her pew, Ruthie was caught off-guard by the unfamiliar configuration. Nor had she heard Brad's instructions. Even worse, the woman before Ruthie, without thinking, handed her the chalice.

Ruthie cradled the chalice close to her chest.

Brad felt sweat trickling from his armpits. Everyone hushed, waiting. Would Ruthie move things along? Or would she embarrass Brad by messing up his carefully planned, innovative spiritual exercise?

Ruthie did nothing. Brad's impatience grew. How could she do this to him? Then, in a flicker of candlelight he suddenly, literally, saw Ruthie Phillips in a different light. He glimpsed the panic in her eyes, could practically hear her asking for guidance, as if saying, "What do I do now, Pahstah Cheese?"

Before he could catch himself, he heard his own voice saying, in a too-kind, too-ministerial, gentle-Jesus voice, "The blood of Christ, Ruthie. Take. Drink."

With that, Ruthie's eyes lit up. She looked into the chalice, put it to her lips, and drank—drained the whole thing, soggy bread crumbs and all!

Brad's jaw dropped in disbelief, but by then she was finished. There stood Ruthie Phillips, empty chalice in hand, proud ear-to-ear smile on her face, huge grape-juice mustache on her upper lip. His choreographed candlelight Communion was ruined. Brad's heart sank.

But then Ruthie glanced around, noticing everyone looking at her.

"Pahstah Cheese," she said loudly in a childlike voice. "Isn't anybody else having juice?"

Brad looked up from the floor, everyone in the circle waiting to see what he'd do.

"It's special Communion tonight, Ruthie," he said, feeling himself relax. Something registered inside. "You see," he said. "Last one to join the circle is guest of honor and gets to drink the juice."

Ruthie grinned.

The boy next to Ruthie gently took the chalice out of her hands, replacing it instead with his lighted Christmas candle. Then he dipped his scrap of dry bread into the empty cup, withdrew it, still dry and unstained, and ate it. Everyone, when they received the empty chalice, did the same, dipped their bread into the cup's emptiness and ate their dry crust.

Eventually it came back around to Brad, who noticed for the first time that the folks in the circle were smiling, not solemn, as they lifted their pieces of bread to their mouths. He'd always believed Communion was supposed to be solemn. Maybe he'd been wrong. People in this circle winked, seemed comfortable, acted relaxed. Something spiritual was going on after all, something Brad hadn't orchestrated, and suddenly the decorations that adorned the sanctuary were lovelier than any he had ever seen. Something shifted inside him.

Oddly enough, Pahstah Cheese ended up the only one without a candle. But he had the empty chalice, which he he rested against his chest. He watched Ruthie Phillips across the circle from him, face lit by the glow of her candle, purple lips singing the carol. Fairhaven Chapel was no cathedral, wasn't at all what he'd thought he wanted or needed. But that night Brad Chesebro found himself warmed and embraced as never before by the spirit of Christmas. Empty chalice in hand, his cup overflowed.

A Christmas Dozen

CHRISTMAS STORIES
TO WARM THE HEART
by STEVE BURT

PLEASE SEND ME THE FOLLOWING:

QUAN.	ITEM	PRICE
_____	Paperback Book ($14.95)	_____
_____	Double cassette read by the author ($15.95)	_____
_____	Double CD read by the author ($16.95)	_____

> *Priority Mail Shipping & handling is $4.50 first item, $2.50 per additional item. Connecticut residents add 6% sales tax.*

SHIPPING _____

SALES TAX _____

TOTAL _____

FREE SHIPPING ON ORDERS OF MORE THAN 10 UNITS

NAME

ADDRESS

CITY   STATE   ZIP

TELEPHONE   FAX   EMAIL

PAYMENT:

☐ Checks payable to: **Burt Creations**
    Mail to: 29 Arnold Place, Norwich, CT 06360

☐ VISA ☐ MasterCard

Cardnumber:_____

Name on card:_____

Exp. Date: _____(mo) _____(year)

◼ **Toll free order phone** 1-866-MyDozen (866-693-6936) (Secure message machine) Give mailing/shipping address, telephone number, MC/Visa name & card number plus expiration date.
◼ **Secure Fax orders:** 860-889-4068. Fill out this form & fax.
◼ **On-line orders:** www.burtcreations.com
                          order@burtcreations.com

O R D E R   F O R M

A Christmas Dozen

CHRISTMAS STORIES
TO WARM THE HEART

by STEVE BURT

PLEASE SEND ME THE FOLLOWING:

QUAN.	ITEM	PRICE
_____	Paperback Book ($14.95)	_____
_____	Double cassette read by the author ($15.95)	_____
_____	Double CD read by the author ($16.95)	_____

> *Priority Mail Shipping & handling is $4.50 first item, $2.50 per additional item. Connecticut residents add 6% sales tax.*

SHIPPING _____
SALES TAX _____
TOTAL _____

FREE SHIPPING ON ORDERS OF MORE THAN 10 UNITS

NAME

ADDRESS

CITY   STATE   ZIP

TELEPHONE   FAX   EMAIL

PAYMENT:

❏ Checks payable to: **Burt Creations**
   Mail to: 29 Arnold Place, Norwich, CT 06360

❏ VISA ❏ MasterCard

Cardnumber:_____
Name on card:_____
Exp. Date: _____(mo) _____(year)

■ **Toll free order phone** 1-866-MyDozen (866-693-6936) (Secure message machine) Give mailing/shipping address, telephone number, MC/Visa name & card number plus expiration date.
■ **Secure Fax orders:** 860-889-4068. Fill out this form & fax.
■ **On-line orders:** www.burtcreations.com
                        order@burtcreations.com